Double Fudge Drowning

The Drunken Pie Café Cozy Mysteries, Book Five

Diana DuMont

CHAPTER ONE

Most people would have been horribly embarrassed to discover chocolate smeared across their upper lip while at a fancy cocktail party. But not Trevor Truman. The jovial salt-and-pepper haired man merely laughed when someone pointed it out to him.

"Oh, dear me," he said. "I must look like a horrible pig who can't control himself and has eaten too much pie. But can you blame me when this double fudge rum pie is the best in the country—if not the world? Izzy has really outdone herself with this recipe."

I blushed when I overheard his words, and quickly turned my face away so I wouldn't accidentally meet his eyes. I didn't feel like getting into any sort of conversation with the slightly tipsy man, even if he was complimenting my baking.

Trevor Truman had had a few too many glasses of champagne. He wasn't drunk, but he was definitely jollier than usual. The man was running for the mayor's office in Sunshine Springs, and had therefore been making quite an effort to get out and attend as many community events as possible. It all seemed a bit disingenuous to me, since I'd never seen him at events like this until he started his campaign. Suddenly, when he wanted people to think he cared about the town of Sunshine Springs, he was everywhere at once.

But if other Sunshine Springs residents were bothered by the fact that he was only now showing up in the community when he needed our votes, they did a good job of hiding it. In fact, most people seemed to be trying to schmooze with him as much as possible. I sighed as I served another piece of double fudge rum pie to one of the party's attendees.

"He knows how to work the crowd. You've got to hand him that," Tiffany Glover said, and I glanced to my left where she stood. Tiffany had been hired to work in my café just a few weeks ago. I'd gotten to know her through a strange set of circumstances, when she'd been accused of murder and I'd been trying to find who the murderer in that case was. Thankfully for me, Tiffany had not turned out to be the murderer, but she *had* turned out to be in need of a job. She had some experience in the restaurant industry, so I'd hired her to come work at my boozy pie shop, the Drunken Pie Café. She'd quickly learned the ropes there, and had been a wonderfully dependable employee. This had been a godsend for me. The holiday season was ramping up, and I wasn't sure how I would have made it without an employee. Besides, she was turning out to be quite a fun person to gossip with.

"Do you really think he'll get elected?" I asked. "Sure, he knows how to work the crowd, but do people really like him all that much? This fountain dedication is the first I've seen of him at these library events."

There had been quite a few library events over the last month. It had all started with a big gala that my best friend Molly, the head librarian, had thrown to celebrate and show off new additions to the library. One of Sunshine Springs' residents had left a huge windfall to the library in his estate, and Molly had been working hard to use the money to improve the library. That first gala had been such a big success that Molly had decided to throw more events. Most of them had been smaller in scale and not as fancy as the initial gala, but the events had all turned out to be quite popular nonetheless. Molly always incorporated live readings from members of the community, and with each event the number of attendees grew.

Tonight's party was a fancier cocktail party that had been set up to christen a giant water fountain that Molly had installed near the front of the library. When she'd first told me of her idea for the fountain, I'd thought it was a bit strange to add a giant fountain to the front of a public library. But Molly had explained that she wanted to set up an area around the fountain with plenty of shade trees and shade umbrellas so that if library patrons wanted to sit outside and read while enjoying the beautiful Northern California weather, they could.

Molly had done a marvelous job with the setup, and I couldn't blame her for beaming with pride as she cut the ribbon at the ribbon-cutting ceremony earlier this evening. That ceremony had officially opened the reading area to the public, and had been followed by a cocktail reception here in the library.

Molly had asked me to help cater the reception by bringing in plenty of dessert pies. My boozy pies had become a favorite in Sunshine Springs since I opened my café several months ago. Anytime I brought pies to a party, I was sure to see them completely eaten up by the end of the night, and tonight was looking to be no exception.

Just then, my grandmother, whom I affectionately called "Grams," sidled up to my pie table and overheard the last of the conversation I'd been having with Tiffany.

"Trevor does seem to have quite a few people eating out of his palm," Grams said. "But I can't imagine that he'll actually get elected. He's far too pompous, and he's too quick to argue with anyone he doesn't agree with."

I turned to look at Grams. She was sporting eccentric, neon-colored hair, as usual. Today, it was neon green. She also wore a bright yellow blouse and a hot pink skirt. She looked like a pack of highlighters gone wrong, but somehow she managed to pull it off. The bright, clashing colors fit her personality well. That was just the way Grams was: never afraid to make a statement.

Still, I was surprised at what she'd just said, and I raised an eyebrow at her. "Really? I haven't heard Trevor fighting with anyone."

"Well, you're about to."

I looked up to see Trevor looking a bit less jovial as he marched angrily across the room, and I frowned as I watched him. "Where's he going with such a ticked-off look on his face?"

"To see Alice," Grams said. "Just watch."

I turned my attention back to Trevor, who looked like he was indeed marching straight toward Alice Warner. Alice was a good friend of mine, and the owner of the Morning Brew Café. She'd been running a café in Sunshine Springs decades longer than I had, and she had graciously helped me many times with tips on how to run a café in our town. She sold coffee and breakfast food, along with Panini's for lunch, so we often sent business each other's way. When someone came into my café looking for something a little more like an actual meal than just pie, I would send them over to Alice. Likewise, if someone came into Alice's café looking for a dessert, she would send them to me.

Alice could be a bit overly anxious about things at times, but that was pretty much her only fault. Overall, she was a sweet, kind café owner whom everyone in Sunshine Springs loved.

Everyone except Trevor, if the scowl on his face could be trusted. I watched as he said something to Alice that I couldn't make out from where I stood. But whatever it was, it clearly made her mad. She spun around with her glass of champagne sloshing around dangerously, and put her face right in his face.

"Why don't you mind your own business? Just because you're running for mayor doesn't mean you have any authority to tell me what to do. And trust me: you're not actually going to get elected. Nobody wants a pompous busybody like you running our town!"

My jaw dropped in shock. I didn't think I'd ever heard Alice say a single mean word to anyone, let alone yell. But here she was, yelling some not-nice things in Trevor's face.

Not that I didn't think he deserved to be yelled at. No matter how much he tried to put on a happy-go-lucky, jovial persona, I couldn't shake the feeling that he was not much more than a pompous lowlife who didn't truly care about anything except his own gain. Still, it surprised me to hear Alice saying things like that. She usually acted so friendly. How had Trevor managed to get her so riled up in just a matter of moments?

Whatever it was they were fighting about, Trevor definitely wasn't backing down. I watched as he got even closer to Alice's face and pointed a threatening finger at her. I noticed then that his cheeks turned a shade of bright pink. Perhaps he was tipsier than I'd originally judged him to be.

Now, he glared at Alice and practically shouted. "You better hope you're wrong, because when I get elected mayor, I'm going to shut you down. That's going to be my first official action: closing the Morning Brew Café. No one who's breaking laws deserves to be running a business in Sunshine Springs."

My jaw dropped even further. What was he talking about? Alice couldn't possibly be breaking any laws. She was the most rule-following person I'd ever met.

Apparently, she agreed with me on that point. She reached up and actually gave Trevor a firm shove in the chest. She was a tiny thing, and he was not exactly small, but he did stumble backward several steps. Perhaps the combination of being surprised along with having drunk too much champagne made it easier for Alice to knock him off balance.

"I'm not doing anything illegal," Alice yelled. "No one's going to elect you as Mayor, and how dare you slander me like that!"

"It's not slander! It's true," Trevor said. Then, he pushed Alice backward just as she'd pushed him.

More gasps rang out across the room, and Mitch McCoy suddenly appeared on the scene. He was wearing a tux and looked quite different from his normal attire, which was a police uniform. He worked as the sheriff in Sunshine Springs, and while I knew he hadn't come here intending to break up fights, he wasn't going to sit around and let Trevor and Alice go at it in the middle of this event.

But Alice wasn't in the mood to be pulled away from this fight. She tried to rush toward Trevor again, and when Mitch held her back, she took her champagne glass and launched all of the champagne inside of it directly at Trevor's face.

For a split second, everyone in the room went completely silent. The only sound was the soft jazz playing in the background. Then, the chaos started anew.

Trevor roared in anger, and started to swing a fist in Alice's direction. I gasped as I watched, and breathed a sigh of relief when Mitch caught Trevor's hand in midair and stopped him from landing a punch in Alice's face.

"What is Trevor doing?" Tiffany asked in a horrified voice. "There's no way he's going to be elected mayor after acting like this! He's out of his mind!"

"He's been out of his mind all week," Grams said.

Before I could ask Grams for more details, I saw Alice shriek and then run off in the direction of the restrooms. It was as though she had just come to her senses and was horrified by the way she was acting. Trevor tried to follow her, but Mitch held him back.

"Oh, no you don't. That's about enough of that," Mitch roared.

Trevor tried to shove him off. "Lay off of me. I just want to go to the men's restroom and clean all of this champagne off of me. Then I'm out of here. It's clear I'm not wanted at this party."

At that, Mitch let him go. Perhaps he thought that if Trevor was going to leave then it was better to just let him.

As Trevor headed toward the restroom, his campaign manager, a lanky man named Cody Stringer—whom I'd always thought was aptly named, since he looked a bit like a string bean—chased after Trevor.

"Mr. Truman! Sir, please calm down. Remember how we talked about always putting your best foot forward?"

But Trevor wasn't interested in heeding his campaign manager's advice. Instead, he looked at Cody and roared, "The only place I want to put my foot is in Alice's face. How dare she humiliate me like this!"

After that, Trevor disappeared around the corner to the restrooms, and I could no longer hear what he was saying. But when I turned to look at Grams and Tiffany, I saw that they were just as shocked at everything that had happened as I was.

"I think he just lost any chance he had at winning the election," Tiffany said.

"Perhaps," Grams said as she reached for a plate to load with a slice of my pie. "But like I was saying earlier, this isn't the first time he and Alice have fought this week. People have forgiven him for it before. This time might not be any different. If you want my take on the matter, I think everyone in Sunshine Springs is actually enjoying the drama a bit."

I turned to look at Grams. "What drama? I haven't heard anything about Alice and Trevor fighting."

I knew that I was a bit behind on the gossip in Sunshine Springs, but I found it hard to believe that I hadn't heard anything about Trevor and Alice fighting if they'd been doing so all week. Of course, I usually got my gossip from Scott Hughes, my best friend Molly's boyfriend. He worked as a package delivery man for Sunshine Springs, and because of that he was always all over town, hearing all the gossip. Whenever he had a delivery to my café, he usually stopped and shared the gossip with me. But in the last few weeks, he'd been so busy with Molly that he'd been rushing through his deliveries and not taking time to stop and gossip. His and Molly's relationship seemed to be getting pretty serious. I was happy for both of them, but I felt completely out of the gossip loop right now.

"What could anyone, especially a candidate for mayor, have to fight over with Alice?" Tiffany asked.

"My thoughts exactly," I said as I turned expectantly toward Grams. "What are they fighting about?"

Grams shrugged as she took a bite of her pie. "I'm not sure all of the exact details. All I know is that Alice has been selling homemade chocolate at her café in an attempt to boost her profits. There are a lot of laws about what kind of homemade goods are allowed to be sold in restaurants. According to Trevor, Alice is violating those laws. Alice says she's not, but he's insistent that she is. They've been fighting like cats and dogs over the issue."

"That's weird," Tiffany said. "Why would Trevor care that much about what Alice is doing? Everyone in town loves her and her café. Going after her doesn't seem like the smartest idea if you want to win an election, whether or not she's technically breaking any of those laws."

"I agree," I said. "There has to be more to the story than that."

Grams shrugged. "You're probably right, but I haven't heard any specifics on why he's so determined to take down Alice's café. I do know that Alice has been having a hard time of it though, which probably explains why she's been getting so riled up at Trevor." Grams lowered her voice and looked around to make sure that only Tiffany and I could hear her. "I've heard that Alice is on the brink of not being able to pay her rent for her café building."

My eyes widened. "What? That doesn't make any sense. She hasn't said anything to me about that. Besides, how is that even possible? She sells out of her café's inventory almost every day."

Grams nodded. "Yes, she sells out, but her prices are too low. She doesn't want to increase her prices even though the cost of ingredients, the cost of rent, and the cost of basically everything has gone up over the last several years. Her prices aren't keeping pace with inflation, and she's slowly drained away her savings to cover the difference."

"She shouldn't do that!" I said. "Of course, no one likes to pay more for things, but everyone loves her food. I'm sure they would understand if she needed to raise her prices a bit to keep from going under."

Grams shrugged. "I agree, but Alice has been adamant about not raising prices. Hence the chocolate to try to make some extra money. Apparently she can make that pretty cheaply and get a good profit on it. But for some reason, Trevor decided to make trouble for her over the fact that it's homemade."

I frowned. "I'm starting to like him even less than I already did. So many people seem so enamored by him, but I don't get what the big deal is. And I can totally see why Alice would be fighting with him if her whole livelihood is being threatened."

My rant was interrupted when I saw Cody, Trevor's campaign manager, come storming from the direction of the restrooms. He looked pale and upset, and I could only imagine how hard dealing with an angry Trevor must have been. I had a feeling that the campaign was beyond repair at this point, and it looked like Cody might have had the same feeling. He went to the bar, threw back a whole glass of champagne in a few big gulps, and then stormed off.

A few moments later, Trevor came storming out of the restrooms and took off in the opposite direction. I hadn't seen Alice yet, and I had a feeling she'd probably hide out in the bathroom for a long time. I was about to make another comment about how futile Trevor's campaign would be at this point, but before I could speak, I felt a firm grasp on my arm. I looked over to see Molly standing next to me, her wide eyes darting around the room as though looking for someone.

"Molly? Who are you looking for?"

She didn't answer me directly. Instead, she leaned in and said, "I have to tell you something. Can you get away from the pie table for a minute?"

I glanced at Tiffany and Grams, who were trying to look like they weren't listening even though I knew they were.

I glanced back at Molly. "I'm sure Tiffany can take over for me for a bit. Why? What's wrong? Is everything going okay with the event?"

But Molly clearly didn't want to say much in front of anyone.

"I need to talk to you alone," she said in a frantic tone. "I have something really important that I absolutely must tell you."

"Go ahead and go with her," Tiffany said, no longer trying to act like she wasn't listening. "I can take care of the pie table by myself. It doesn't require that much work to slice pies and hand them out."

I nodded my thanks, and said goodbye to Grams. I could tell from the glint in Grams' eye that she wanted to know what this was all about, but she knew better than to try to ask right now. She would bide her time until I was back, and then she would corner me to ask me what it was my best friend had so urgently needed. Whether or not I would tell her would depend on what sort of issue this actually was. But if the look on Molly's face could be trusted, she had something quite serious to tell me. I hoped that it wasn't anything too bad, and that everything with the event tonight was going okay. I knew Molly worked really hard on these parties.

There was only one way to find out for sure, though. I followed Molly out into the night, thankful that the November evening wasn't too terribly chilly here in Northern California.

CHAPTER TWO

As soon as I walked out of the library, Sprinkles, my Dalmatian who had been waiting outside, came running up to me. He wasn't allowed in the main area of the library since they had a strict no pets policy. Molly had offered to let him stay in a back room so that he wouldn't have to be out in the cold evening air, but Sprinkles had made it clear that he preferred to be outside.

Now, he excitedly raced up to me, wagging his tail and sniffing my hands in search of pie. I had promised I'd bring him a piece when the event was over, and he looked at me in a huff when he realized that there was no pie in my hands. I laughed at him.

"The event's not over yet, boy. I'm just out here to talk to Molly for a moment." I turned to look at Molly expectantly. "So? What was it you wanted to tell me?"

Molly looked around nervously, as though worried someone would be listening in. She was about to speak when a twig snapped a few yards away, and I saw a dark shadow slinking through the trees in front of the new fountain.

Molly jumped, and then shook her head. "Let's walk a little ways away. I don't want anyone to hear this. That's probably just someone out for a smoke or some fresh air, but I want to make sure you're the only one who knows what I'm about to tell you."

I nodded, but shivered slightly—and not from the cold. It wasn't like Molly to be so secretive. What could possibly have her so tensed up?

We walked away from the library for a minute before Molly finally stopped and turned toward me to speak. It was then that I saw a giddy smile on her face, and I knew that whatever this was, it was actually good news. Sprinkles ran around us, sniffing every blade of grass, every bush, and every rock. He was happy to have company and to be stretching his legs on this beautiful moonlit night, and for a moment Molly and I both watched him in silence. But then, I couldn't hold back my curiosity any longer.

"Molly?" I prompted. "What's going on?"

She squealed in delight. "I think Scott's going to propose tonight!"

I couldn't hide the shock on my face. "Really? What makes you think so? You guys haven't even been dating all that long."

"I know we haven't been dating long, but it's not like we don't already know each other well. We've been good friends for most of our lives. Once we started dating and realized that we have a lot of the same goals and want a lot of the same things out of life, it doesn't make sense to delay our future just for some arbitrary need to have dated for a certain amount of time. We've been dancing around the subject and discussing that we'd like to get married sooner rather than later. We haven't made any concrete plans, but I have a feeling he's going to propose sometime soon. He's been dropping hints for the last few days that this is going to be the best holiday season ever. Maybe he just means it's going to be great because we're dating, but perhaps he means more?"

"Perhaps," I said slowly. I didn't want my friend to get her hopes up if she was reading too much into things. It was quite possible that Scott merely meant it was going to be the best holiday season ever because they were now dating. Without something more, I wasn't so sure that this was a sign of an imminent proposal. But then, Molly plowed ahead with more information.

"It's not just the comments about the holiday season, either. He's been acting strange all night tonight. He keeps reaching into his pocket obsessively, like he wants to check that something is still there. Do you think it's possible that it's a ring box?"

This sounded slightly more promising than the vague "best holidays ever" comment. I opened my mouth to reassure Molly that it at least sounded promising, and that I hoped it was true that Scott was going to propose, even though it was hard for me to wrap my head around the idea. I had barely gotten to the point of wrapping my head around the idea that they were dating, and now they might be getting engaged?

It was a lot to take in, but anyone who knew Molly couldn't deny that she was extremely happy these days. And if being with Scott made her this happy, then I hoped that things continued to go well in their relationship.

But before I could get the words out, we were interrupted by someone running toward us. My heart leapt in my throat as I turned toward the sound, and then I felt a sense of panic overtake me when I saw that the person running toward us was Norman Wade, the current city mayor. He looked completely panicked himself, which I had never seen before. He usually acted so calm and collected as he went about his business as the city mayor.

He did not look calm and collected right now. His suit jacket was crumpled, and his tie was coming undone. His hair was a complete mess, and even in the dim light of the moon, I could see that his cheeks were flushed red from the exertion of running.

"Norman? What's wrong?" I asked.

"You have to come! You have to come quick! Oh, it's so awful!"

Molly and I looked at each other in confusion, and Sprinkles started running in circles around us, barking as though understanding that something here was not going well.

"Norman, slow down," Molly said. "Tell us what's happened."

Norman was inconsolable. "It's so awful! You have to come!"

So much for leadership, I thought as I watched him wringing his hands. *Shouldn't the mayor be the one remaining calm in a crisis?*

And whatever this was, it must be a crisis. The look on the mayor's face wasn't something you'd expect to see from a simple inconvenience like the party running out of pie.

"Where do we need to come?" I asked him, trying to make sense of this. "What's wrong?"

"There's someone bobbing in the fountain!"

"Bobbing in the fountain?" Molly asked. "What in the world are you talking about?"

Norman wrung his hands some more. "I went outside for some fresh air, and I thought I'd get a closer look at the new fountain while I was out there. I thought it would be nice to have some peace and quiet after all the hullabaloo between Trevor and Alice. But when I walked to the fountain, I saw someone bobbing in there. It's so awful!"

Everything suddenly clicked into place, and I stared at Norman for just a moment more. "Wait a minute. Are you telling me that there is someone in the fountain who is possibly drunk and you just left them there?"

Norman sniffled and nodded, apparently not seeing why this was such a terrible thing.

"Why in the world didn't you pull them out?" I yelled over my shoulder as I took off running toward the fountain.

Thankfully, even though I was wearing a fancy cocktail dress, I was not wearing heels. I was more of a flats kind of girl, and usually only wore heels to weddings and funerals. Even a fancy cocktail party at the library for my best friend wasn't enough for me to break out the heels, especially when I was going to be on my feet serving pie all evening. I had never been as thankful for my love of flats as I was at that moment, running across the library's concrete driveway back toward the fountain.

I hoped that whomever Norman had left in the fountain hadn't drowned. What kind of mayor leaves a drunken person alone in a body of water?

When I arrived at the fountain, my heart dropped. There, in the water, there was indeed a person bobbing. A man in evening dress, to be exact. But he was bobbing face down, and didn't look like he was moving beyond the gentle rocking back and forth that the small waves from the fountain caused.

This was no drunken person playing around. This was a drunken person who had drowned. As much as I hated to do it, I ran up to the fountain and jumped in, then flipped the man over. I had to check whether he was still alive, and see if there was any way to still save him, even though things didn't look good.

When I flipped the man over, I let out a shriek.

It was Trevor. His face was frozen in a sort of surprised expression— the same sort of expression that he seemed to be so good at when he was alive.

But he was no longer alive. After just a moment of double-checking his pulse to be sure, I looked up and shook my head at Molly and Norman.

"One of you better go get Mitch," I said. "We have a bit of a situation here."

CHAPTER THREE

Before I could stop Norman or suggest that perhaps he should use a little bit of discretion, he ran toward the library's entrance screaming at the top of his lungs.

"Help! There's a drowned man out here! Help!"

Molly groaned, and took off running after him.

I stood awkwardly in the fountain, with the spray from the water quickly soaking my hair and dress. I must have looked like a drowned rat, which definitely had not been the look I was going for when I got ready for the party this evening. But I wasn't that worried about appearances at the moment. What I was worried about was the fact that one of our candidates for mayor was now permanently out of the running.

I shivered as I looked down at Trevor, and realized then that Sprinkles was running around the perimeter of the fountain, barking at me. Sprinkles probably wanted me to get out of the fountain, and I wanted the same thing. It wasn't exactly pleasant getting soaked on this November evening. Even though Northern California wasn't exactly known for its severe winters, it still wasn't what you would call warm right now, especially when you were soaking wet.

I also didn't enjoy being mere feet away from a dead body. But I would feel like a horrible person if I left Trevor here on his own. It was so cold and dark. It seemed wrong to leave him alone like that. So I stood there, feeling awkward and exposed and very alone. Finally, to my great relief, I saw Mitch running out of the library's entrance.

He headed straight for the fountain, and when he saw me standing in there, he didn't hesitate to leap over the edge and jump in, even though he was also wearing expensive evening clothes.

"Izzy! What happened here? Why are you standing in the water? Come on out. You're going to catch pneumonia."

He pulled me toward the edge of the fountain, with only a quick glance back at Trevor's floating body. That's when I noticed that I was shaking violently. I wasn't sure whether it was from the cold, or just from the shock of seeing Trevor like that, but once I realized how overwhelming the moment was, I couldn't stop the tears from forming in my eyes.

I saw that Molly was right behind Mitch. Mitch turned to Molly and asked if she had warm clothes or a blanket I could use. I only half-understood what they were saying, because I was in so much shock by that time.

When Molly took my hand to guide me back toward the library building, I went willingly. As I walked toward the building, though, I saw numerous people coming out. Norman was leading the crowd, but right after him came pretty much everyone else from the party. I saw Theo, the owner of the Sunshine Springs Winery, who was a good friend of mine and also a would-be suitor—although thus far I'd rebuffed all of his efforts to win my heart. When he saw me, he immediately changed directions and made a beeline for Molly and me, but Molly waved him away.

"Don't worry about her. I'll get her some warm clothes and get her taken care of. You go help Mitch. I have a feeling he's going to need help controlling this crowd."

Theo looked like he was going to protest, but then Grams came up behind him as well. She touched his arm lightly and gave him a gentle push toward the fountain. "Molly's right. Mitch needs you. I'll help Molly with Izzy."

Theo gave one last glance back toward me, and I nodded at him, encouraging him to go. I was in good hands with Molly and Grams taking care of me, and there wasn't much he could do to help beyond what they could do.

Reluctantly, Theo nodded and turned to head toward the fountain. As he did, I saw several other faces in the crowd that I recognized. Tiffany was running out of the library, her hands clasped over her face in shock. She didn't even notice me as she ran in the direction of the fountain. Several women in cocktail dresses screamed, and one even fainted. Almost no one saw me. Most people were too busy focusing on the fountain to notice me hobbling along.

Then, I saw Cody come running out, charging through the crowd faster than everyone. He was yelling something about the fact that he couldn't believe someone would do this, and that he bet it was Norman who had drowned Trevor.

It wasn't until that moment that I had considered the fact that Trevor's drowning might not have been accidental. In my horror over the whole situation, I had just assumed that he'd had too much champagne, had angrily stormed out of the library after his fight with Alice, and had drunkenly fallen into the fountain.

But what if that wasn't what happened? What if someone had given him a little bit of "help" in falling into the fountain?

Apparently, Molly had just had the same revelation, because she paused and looked back toward Cody with a look of horror on her face. Then she looked at me.

"You think that's possible?" she asked.

Cody's ranting was growing louder, and now I could clearly hear his yelling over even the din of the crowd. "Of course, Norman isn't here anymore! The coward ran off before anyone could realize he was the one who killed Trevor!"

Surprised, I swung my head back and forth over the crowd. I'd seen Norman just a few minutes earlier, but now, Cody was right: Norman was nowhere to be seen. Had he escaped because he'd killed Trevor? Had it not been just a coincidence that Norman had been the one who'd found Trevor? Had he actually been the one to kill him, and then had tried to make it look like an accident to cover things up?

I glanced back toward Mitch, and saw that his face was set in a hard line as he yelled at the crowd to step back. Theo was trying to help him, but everyone was ignoring them and shouting out questions about whether Norman had drowned Trevor. But then, one voice shouted so loudly above the crowd that everyone heard it clearly. I didn't know who it was that shouted, because it was impossible to tell amidst the din of so many people yelling, but somehow the words rang through loud and clear.

"What about Alice? She's not around, either? Who's to say she didn't drown him?"

An eerie silence fell over the crowd. "Good point," someone said, but other than that no one spoke.

I felt my stomach turn. There was no way, was there? Alice was one of the sweetest, kindest people I knew. Even if she'd been disagreeing with Trevor, she never would have drowned him.

But the silence hung heavy as everyone searched across the crowd, looking for any sign of Alice.

She wasn't there.

Then Sprinkles suddenly started growling and barking. I nearly jumped out of my skin at the loud sound, and turned to see my Dalmatian running toward the parking lot. To my great surprise, Alice's car was pulling out of its parking spot. Gasps rang out as everyone watched Alice rev up her engine and screech away.

I glanced back at Mitch, who was shaking his head in disbelief. The last thing I heard before the crowd started roaring again was Mitch speaking to one of his officers.

"Smith, you'd better go chase down Alice."

Officer Smith nodded, ran to his patrol car, and disappeared into the night with his lights blazing and siren blaring.

CHAPTER FOUR

About thirty minutes later, I was warm and dry, dressed in a "Friends of the Library" sweatshirt and a pair of extra sweatpants from Molly's gym bag. My hair looked like an unruly, frizzy mess, but at least it was dry. Not that it mattered much what my hair looked like at this point. The party had clearly come to an end.

I watched as Molly and Grams started to clean up as best they could. Outside, the chaos continued. I went to peek through the front door, and I saw that a yellow crime scene tape had been set up around the perimeter of the fountain. The crowd had thinned somewhat, but there were still plenty of people there trying to get a look at the body floating in the fountain. I shivered, and looked away. Why would anyone want to see that on purpose?

I was about to close the door when I saw a commotion on one side of the crowd. A redheaded woman was waving her hands wildly, trying to fight her way to the front of the crowd and then through the crime scene tape. Mitch's officers held her back as best they could, but she looked inconsolable.

Molly must have wondered what I was looking at, because she came and joined me at the window. "Is that Sydney Joyner?"

I squinted, and then nodded. "It sure looks like it. She's going a little crazy out there."

As Molly and I watched, I saw Scott rushing up to Sydney and trying to calm her down. But she seemed inconsolable, and continued to wave her hands wildly.

Grams joined us at the window, then clucked her tongue and shook her head sadly. "It's no wonder she's upset. She worked as the head of the elections committee. She was pretty close to all of the candidates, since you had to be in contact with them so much for her job. She probably knew

Trevor pretty well, so I'm sure it's a shock to see him floating dead in the fountain."

Molly winced and turned away. "I wasn't Trevor's biggest fan, but I can't believe he's actually gone. What a horrible way to go. Whether or not this was foul play or an accident, that can't be a pleasant way to die."

I turned away as well, and headed back toward my pie table to start packing things up. Molly tried to wave me away, and I knew she was about to tell me she'd take care of things. But I shook my head.

"You've had just as much of a shock as I have," I said. "I'm not going to leave you alone to clean all of this up by yourself, especially since a good portion of the party cleanup is my pie table. I'll at least take care of that."

"Fine, but only the pie table. Then you need to get out of here and get some rest."

I merely grunted in response. I had no intentions of leaving once the pie table was cleaned up. I would stay and help with everything, and I knew Grams would as well. In fact, Grams was already starting to pack away the leftover bottles of champagne.

For a few minutes, we worked in silence. I suppose none of us were quite sure what to say. I don't think any of us wanted to bring up the fact that Alice had suspiciously driven away. I couldn't believe that she would actually have killed Trevor, no matter how much they were fighting. But if she wasn't somehow at fault, then why had she run off like she did? I couldn't bear to actually ask the question aloud, and apparently neither could anyone else in the room.

The silence was short-lived, however, because a few moments later Scott came bursting into the room. Despite everything going on, Molly's face lit up when she saw him. She ran to him and embraced him, and he kissed the top of her head.

I smiled at the sweetness of it, and felt a small pang of loneliness. It had been a long time since I'd felt loved in the way that Scott and Molly loved each other. After a nasty divorce, I'd purposely kept all men at arms' length. I wasn't ready for the responsibility and risk of a relationship, but I did miss the good parts of being connected to someone that closely.

"Isn't it awful!" Molly exclaimed, her voice somewhat muffled as she buried it into Scott's chest. "I can't believe Trevor is dead. Do you think it's true that it wasn't an accident, and somebody actually pushed him in?"

"I don't know," Scott said in a weary voice. "I heard Mitch telling one of his officers that they need to check for signs of a struggle, but I don't have any more information than that. I came in here to check if you're alright, and to let you know that Mitch is looking for someone to take Sydney Joyner home. If it's okay with you, I think I'll offer to help him out and do that. She's pretty inconsolable at the moment, and Mitch and his officers have enough to deal with just trying to keep the crowds at bay. I don't want them to have to worry about taking care of her, too."

Molly nodded. "Of course you should take her. I'm fine here. Izzy and Grams are helping me clean up, so I'm sure it won't take that long. Obviously, this party is over." She buried her head in her hands, and moaned. "What a disaster! This definitely isn't how I wanted this party to go. Now all anyone is going to think of when they use the fountain area is how somebody died in that fountain."

I winced as I listened to her. I certainly hoped that people would still use the fountain installation. So much money and effort had been put into planning that fountain and its surrounding shade and seating areas. But I feared that Molly was right. For some time, at least, it was likely that most people would only think of Trevor's death when they thought of that fountain.

I didn't want to say this and crush her hopes further, though, so I piped in and said, "I'm sure it will probably be shock for a while, but that shock will eventually wear off. The fountain and the area surrounding it is beautiful. Eventually, the memory of this tragedy will fade, and people will find beauty in the fountain again."

Molly gave me a grateful glance and sniffled. "You really think so?"

"I know so."

Molly nodded, and smiled bravely up at Scott. "You should go ahead and take Sydney home. I'm sure the trauma of this night will take a long time for her to move past. I'll be fine here, so don't worry about me."

Scott pulled Molly close for one more hug, and then left with a promise to call her when he was done driving Sydney home.

As soon as Scott had left, I went over to Molly.

"Are you sure you're okay?" I asked. "I know this isn't the way you were hoping this night would turn out."

I didn't want to say anything specifically about a possible proposal in case Molly still didn't want Grams or anyone else to know about that.

But Molly sniffled and looked over at Grams with a sheepish smile. "It's okay. I don't mind if Grams knows."

"Knows what?" Grams asked, looking up from where she was on her hands and knees, scrubbing a red wine spill off the library's floor. Thankfully, the spill had landed on the hardwood instead of on the carpet. I had to admire the fact that my grandmother at her age seemed to have no issue being down on her hands and knees to scrub the floor. I hoped I aged as well as she had.

Molly smiled at her. "I thought that perhaps Scott was going to propose to me tonight. Maybe it sounds silly, because we haven't been dating that long. But he's been dropping hints, and he knew this was a big night for me."

Grams grinned at Molly and laughed. "Oh that? That's not news.

Everyone in town is just waiting for Scott to man up and actually ask the question. It's obvious you two are meant to be."

Molly blinked in surprise, as did I.

"Really?" I asked. "How did everyone else in town realize that Scott was on the edge of proposing to my best friend, but it totally went over my head?"

Grams winked at me. "You have to understand: when you've been around as long as I have, you recognize true love when you see it. All the older ladies in Sunshine Springs are just waiting for the announcement." Then Grams turned and looked at Molly. "I am really sorry that it didn't happen tonight, though. You might have been right that that's what Scott was planning, but obviously under the circumstances, his plans must have changed."

Molly smiled gratefully at Grams, then turned to smile at me as well. "It's alright. If he was going to propose, he still will. He'll just find a new time to do it. Perhaps a romantic proposal for Thanksgiving dinner?"

I giggled at the hopeful tone in her voice. "Scott's a good man, and he clearly loves you very much. I'm sure that however he chooses to propose, it will be special. And don't worry about the fountain. I'm sure people will still use it. This night may not have gone as we hoped, but there are still a lot of good things to look forward to in the future. Sunshine Springs is still a great community. And we'll all pull together after this to be even stronger than before."

"That's the truth!" Grams piped in. "We've never let tragedies or setbacks bring us down for long here in Sunshine Springs. And anyway, Izzy, aren't you excited that there is a potential new murder case for you to solve?"

I looked over at Grams and groaned. "No! I don't want to be involved in another murder case. I'm done with that."

Grams raised an eyebrow at me. Without her even saying anything, I knew she was telling me that she had her doubts about whether I was actually done with investigating murder cases.

I threw my hands in the air in frustration. "Okay, okay! If I'm honest, I am a little bit curious about what happened. But Mitch is right when he tells me that these cases are dangerous. Besides, the holiday season is about to be in full swing. I need to focus on my pie shop and not on detective work. I didn't even know Trevor all that well, so I don't feel any obligation to find justice for him. Mitch can handle that, and I'm sure Mitch won't be asking for my help this time like he did on the last case."

I crossed my arms as if that settled it, but Grams merely made a "hmph" sound and turned back to scrubbing the floor. In exasperation, I went back to packing up the pie from my pie table. Molly said nothing, apparently not wanting to get involved in telling me whether I should or shouldn't help investigate Trevor's death. I knew Molly always felt conflicted about these things. She didn't want me to put myself in harm's way, but she also had a curious streak and enjoyed helping me in my sleuthing efforts.

Regardless of what either of them thought, I was too busy for detective work right now. Besides, we didn't even know for sure that Trevor's death had been a murder. It was entirely possible, despite Cody's angry ranting, that this truly had been just an accident. We'd all seen how much champagne Trevor had been drinking. It wouldn't have been that much of a surprise if he'd drunkenly fallen face-first into the fountain and never come out.

I took my frustrations out on my leftover pies, being a little too rough as I shoved them into pie boxes. Because tonight's event had ended earlier than expected, I actually had quite a bit of pie leftover. I never sold day-old pie at my café, so all of these pies would either be given away or tossed.

I was sure Sprinkles would be happy that so much pie remained. Right now, he was sitting right next to the entrance door and watching me eagerly. Molly had said he could come inside as long as he didn't stray from right by the door, and he was all too happy to take the opportunity to scope out what leftover food he might be lucky enough to snack on. As I looked up at him, he thumped his tail a few times and turned his lips up in an adorable doggy smile. I couldn't help but smile back. He was quite an expert at looking adorable in his quest to get more treats.

But then, I saw that Sprinkles' tail wasn't the only thing moving: the door behind him was opening. I looked on with curiosity, wondering who was coming into the library now. I hadn't looked out the window for quite some time, but surely by this point the crowds around the fountain must have dispersed. After the coroner had come and taken Trevor's body for an autopsy, there wouldn't have been much left to see.

Molly and Grams also turned around at the sound of the door opening. Then, we all gasped when we saw who had just stepped into the library.

There, with the light of the entrance lamps glowing yellow behind her, stood Alice—looking more shocked and frightened than I'd ever seen her.

CHAPTER FIVE

Molly and I exchanged a glance, as if silently asking each other what the best way to handle this situation might be.

Grams coughed awkwardly, and I saw that she was slowly standing from where she had still been cleaning up the floor. "Alice," she said in a surprisingly calm tone of voice, considering that we had all seen Alice running from the police just a half an hour ago.

I wondered if Alice had gotten away, or if the police had caught up with her and then let her go, realizing that there hadn't been any foul play against Trevor.

From the way Alice was shaking, I had a feeling that she hadn't been actually cleared by the police, but rather had escaped them. A moment later, she broke into sobs, which I felt confirmed my suspicions even more.

"Please! I need help! The police are after me for Trevor's murder, but I didn't kill him!"

She started sobbing even harder, and I exchanged one more glance with Molly before walking over to her and putting my arm around her.

"Come on," I said gently. "Come sit down and take a few deep breaths. I'm sure there's a way to sort this all out."

Alice wailed. "I can't handle a murder investigation right now! My café is already in ruins. I'm not making enough profit, and Trevor was doing his best to shut me down. He'd already tried to give me as much bad publicity as possible, and if I'm the subject of an investigation into his murder, it's going to be even more bad publicity. You have to help me!"

"Alice, calm down," I urged. "For one thing, we don't even know that Trevor was murdered. It's possible that his death could have been an accident."

Alice looked at me like I was crazy. "Oh, come on. Do you really think he would have drowned in a fountain like that? That fountain isn't that deep, and he was a big guy. He could've easily climbed out."

I shrugged. "He had been drinking quite a bit, and it doesn't take much water to actually drown."

"Ugh," Molly piped in just then. "I hate to be the bearer of bad news, but it sounds like Alice is right." She held up her phone. "Scott just texted me to say that he heard that the preliminary findings from the coroner's office suggest foul play."

Alice wailed even harder at this, and I frowned. I had no idea how Scott had gotten that information, but I knew that if he was texting it to Molly, then it was probably reliable. Scott was better at getting town gossip than almost anyone else in Sunshine Springs. The only person who beat him out in that feat was possibly Sophia Reed, the owner of the local hair salon. If Scott said that foul play was involved, then that was probably the truth.

Still, even though that was bad news, I couldn't imagine that Alice would actually be a serious suspect. She was one of those people who would carry a spider out of her café and set it free instead of killing it. She quite literally would not hurt a fly.

Of course, I *had* seen her shoving Trevor earlier that evening. But she hadn't seriously hurt him, and I couldn't blame her for being angry with him. Not when he was doing his best to bring down her café, and had been slandering her in front of everyone. I reached out to put another comforting hand on her shoulder.

"Alice, calm down. We'll get this sorted out. I promise. I believe you that you would never have hurt Trevor, but you have to talk to Mitch. He has a duty to investigate any possible lead on a murder investigation. It's nothing personal that he's coming after you. He's just obligated to take a statement from you, and the sooner you go and give him that statement, the better it will be for you."

My words didn't seem to comfort Alice at all. She looked up at me and shook her head in despair. "Everyone's going to think I did it. Everyone saw me fighting with him. You have to help me, Izzy! You know how to solve murder cases! Please, can you find the true murderer and clear my name?"

I held up my hands in a gesture of surrender. "Whoa, whoa, whoa. I am *not* a professional detective. You need to talk to Mitch, and tell him everything you know. He'll be fair with you, but I'm not getting involved in any more murder cases."

Alice sniffed, and started sobbing harder. "But, Izzy," she said between sobs. "I trust you. You've done such a great job of finding the true culprit in so many other murder cases. Everyone in Sunshine Springs knows that you're the best detective around. No offense to Mitch, but you have a natural talent for this. Please. I need your help. You're one of my best friends, and surely you understand how important my café is to me. If you don't help me, and this investigation drags on forever, my café—my life's work—will be lost."

I chewed my lower lip for a moment. I felt guilty not helping Alice, but I really didn't want to get involved in another case. How could I say no, though? Alice was right. She was one of my best friends, and I did know how important her café was to her. I decided to just ask a few questions without committing to actually helping her.

"Let's just calmly think through this, okay? Maybe you'll feel better if we talk through who else might have been responsible for Trevor's death. Do you know of anyone else who was fighting with him?"

Alice looked up at me with tears streaming down her face, but she managed to calm down enough to think through my question. "My guess would be Norman. I know it seems odd that our mayor would kill someone, but I did see Trevor and Norman fighting quite often. Trevor managed to get under a lot of people's skin, but especially under Norman's. A few days ago, after a heated conversation with Trevor in my café, Norman seemed especially distressed. In fact, I've never seen Norman fighting with someone the way he fought with Trevor that day."

"What were they fighting about?" I asked.

Alice shrugged. "I don't know. They were speaking in hushed enough tones when actually discussing the issue that I don't know what the issue was. By the time they were at the point of yelling, the conversation had evolved into vague insults, so I never learned what the specific complaint was. All I know is that they made quite a scene. Norman stormed out, and Trevor stayed behind fuming. Several minutes later, Cody Stringer arrived for a meeting with Trevor about the campaign. Trevor was still so angry that he just about bit poor Cody's head off."

I considered all of this. "Do you think Norman would actually kill someone, though?"

More tears escaped Alice's eyes. "I don't know. I wouldn't have thought so, but it wasn't me, so who else could it have been? I do know that Norman had been complaining to others in the café that he felt his hold on the mayor's office was slipping. Trevor had been running quite a robust public relations campaign, and there were quite a few people in Sunshine Springs who were starting to question whether it might be good to have some fresh blood in the mayor's office."

I winced when Alice said the words "fresh blood," and she seemed to realize that it might be an awkward phrase to use given the circumstances.

"You know what I meant," she hurriedly said. "Not literal blood, but just a new face…"

I tried to smile reassuringly at her. "I know what you meant. Don't worry. Listen, I'm not going to promise to actually take on the case, but I will at least talk to Mitch about it."

Alice's face lit up, but I held up a hand to stop her before she could say anything else.

"But you have to promise to at least turn yourself in and make a statement."

Alice's face fell. "I can't talk to the police. I just can't! What if they charge me? What if they throw me in jail?"

Molly came over and sat with us, putting a reassuring hand on Alice's arm.

"Listen," Molly said. "Mitch isn't going to throw you in jail without rock solid evidence that you committed a murder. Since I'm sure he doesn't have that, because I'm sure you didn't actually commit the murder, you'll be fine. If you keep running from him, all you're doing is making yourself look guiltier. He's eventually going to catch you, so you're just making this harder on everyone and making yourself look worse by not talking to him right away."

Grams came and sat with us as well. "Alice, dear. Molly and Izzy are right. Let Izzy drive you down to the station and talk to Mitch. The sheriff is a good man, and he's fair. He has to do his job, but he won't throw you in jail or cause any more trouble for you than necessary. Besides, if you're worried about your café going under, hiding from Mitch is the worst thing you can do. How are you going to run your café if you're trying to avoid Mitch? You can't exactly walk into work and expect the police not to come looking for you there."

Alice considered this, then slowly nodded. "You're all right. It just feels so unfair that I have to go give a statement about this when I didn't do anything to Trevor. He was the one attacking me! I was just defending myself when I threw the champagne at him. And I never would have thrown him in the fountain! Look what a giant of a man he was, and how small I am. Does anyone seriously think I could have actually pushed him into the water?"

I didn't bother to tell Alice that Trevor had probably been drunk enough for almost anyone to push him into the water. I figured that wasn't a helpful thing to point out at the moment, and I wanted to keep her calm enough that I could actually convince her to go down to the station. So, I just smiled and gave her shoulder another squeeze.

"I know it feels unfair," I said. "But Mitch will take care of everything as quickly as possible. Now, come on. I'll drive you down to the station and we'll get this all taken care of so you can go home and get some rest. That's the best thing you can do for yourself right now."

Alice sniffled and nodded, then stood on shaky legs to let me lead her out to my car. Sprinkles followed us and jumped into the backseat of my car. As we drove away, he stuck his head into the front seat and rested his muzzle reassuringly on Alice's shoulder. She seemed comforted by this, and

I was glad of that.

But I myself felt a bit uneasy. Alice didn't seem like a likely murderer, but neither did Norman. But if neither of them had killed Trevor, then who could have possibly done it? Was there another murderer running loose on the streets of Sunshine Springs?

As I drove quickly through the dark streets of Sunshine Springs toward the police station, I had a feeling that I was about to be entangled deeply in another murder case, whether I liked it or not.

CHAPTER SIX

There were several cars at the police station when we arrived, which was unusual for that time of night. Unless there was something going on—like, say, a murder case—most of the station's employees didn't work past five P.M.

But tonight, it looked like all of the employees at the station were there. My heart sank when I saw this. Mitch didn't tolerate people hanging around the station just looking for gossip. That meant that if his employees were here, they were actually working. And if that many employees were actually working, then Trevor's death was definitely a murder case and not an accidental drowning. How could the police really know that so soon, though?

I wasn't sure, but I tried to smile and put on a brave face for Alice's sake. She looked like she was about to bolt as I pulled into a parking spot, so I tried to speak reassuringly to her.

"Just remember to stay calm," I advised. "Mitch will take your statement, and then my guess is he'll let you go home and just say he'll be in touch. Don't try to overthink what you're saying. Just tell Mitch the truth, and I promise everything is going to be fine."

Alice still looked like she was about to run, but at that moment, Sprinkles whined and reached forward to put a paw on her arm. This seemed to calm her, and I gave my Dalmatian a grateful look. As stubborn as he could be sometimes, I had to admit that he always came through when I truly needed him.

I quickly got out and put my arm around Alice to help her into the station before she changed her mind. Sprinkles followed us to the front door, and walked straight into the reception area behind us. Normally, the receptionist would have told him he had to wait outside. But tonight, no one seemed to notice him. He sat quietly in the corner as if he knew that if he just remained quiet, he'd likely be able to stay.

Perhaps the reason the receptionist didn't notice Sprinkles was that she was too shocked at the sight of Alice. Her eyes widened, and she opened her mouth as if she was going to say something before promptly shutting it again.

"C-c-can I help you?" she finally stammered.

I smiled warmly at her, trying to act like it was a completely normal thing for me to walk into the police station with someone connected to a potential murder case. I almost laughed when I realized that, actually, it *was* almost normal. I'd been involved in so many murder cases now that I doubted Mitch or anyone would think twice about the fact that I'd suddenly shown up with Alice.

"We're here to see Mitch," I said calmly. "Do you think he's available?"

"Y-y-yes," she stammered, and grabbed for the phone so quickly that she knocked the receiver onto the floor. She quickly picked it back up and paged Mitch.

Less than a minute later, he appeared in the reception area. I could tell that he was trying to act calm and collected, but he couldn't completely hide from me the fact that he was shocked to see Alice here.

"Izzy?" he asked. He didn't say anything more than that, but I understood what he was actually asking. He wanted to know how in the world I'd found Alice and convinced her to show up at the station when his own officers clearly hadn't been able to keep up with her and bring her in.

Now was not the time to actually ask me those questions, though. The most important priority here was to get Alice in and get a statement from her before she bolted again—and if the look on her face was any indication, she wanted nothing more in that moment than to bolt. I kept my arm firmly around her shoulders, not only for comfort but also to encourage her not to run.

Without much small talk, Mitch led us back to an interview room. He sat down with another one of his officers and prepared to take a statement, but first looked at me. "Izzy, perhaps you should leave us alone for a few minutes so we can talk to Alice?"

Before I could say anything, Alice slammed her fist down on the table. "No! Izzy stays or I don't talk."

Mitch shifted uncomfortably in his seat. "I understand you're upset, Alice. It's just that we don't usually allow anyone except the person of interest and his or her lawyer in the room while a statement is being taken."

"Izzy is my lawyer!" Alice exclaimed.

Now it was my turn to shift uncomfortably in my seat. "Alice, I'm not actually your lawyer. Yes, I used to be a lawyer. But I was a contracts lawyer, not a criminal lawyer. And besides, I'm not working as a lawyer anymore. I'm just here as your friend."

"Fine, whatever," Alice said as she set her expression in a hard line. "But whatever Izzy wants to call herself, I'm not giving a statement unless she's here. That's my offer. Take it or leave it."

Mitch gave me a long-suffering look, and I shrugged as if to say "What can I do?"

And what could I do? I wasn't the one who had decided I needed to be here. Mitch should just be grateful that Alice was here and talking at all. He seemed to understand that, because he didn't argue further.

"Fine. Then let's get on with this. Alice, you do understand that we're asking you questions in regards to a criminal investigation? You have a right to have a lawyer here—an actual criminal lawyer. You don't have to speak, but anything you do say may be used against you in a court of law."

Alice's face paled as Mitch continued to explain her rights, and I nervously tapped my foot, hoping that she wasn't going to change her mind and run out of there. Thankfully, she stayed and agreed to give her statement. Mitch asked her where she had been at the time of Trevor's death. She explained to him that she hadn't seen Trevor again after she threw champagne in his face and ran into the restroom.

"I stayed in the bathroom a long time," she said. "I was so embarrassed by the way I'd acted and by the way that Trevor had yelled at me in front of everyone that I didn't want to come out and face anyone again. I was hiding in a stall inside the women's restroom, waiting for the party to be over so I could leave without having to face everyone. But after I'd been in there for a little while, I heard a bunch of commotion outside, and some screaming. When I came out to see what had happened, I saw people running outside, and everyone yelling that Trevor had been found dead in the fountain."

Mitch frowned as he made some notes on his notepad, and then he tapped his pen a few times on the table before looking back up at Alice. "Did anyone see you in the restroom while you were in there?"

"No," Alice replied. "Like I said, I was hiding inside the stall because I was embarrassed and didn't want to see anybody."

Mitch's frown deepened, and so did mine. This didn't exactly look good for Alice. She'd been missing during the whole time that the murder had taken place, with no witnesses to verify where she was. Mitch didn't focus on this fact for the moment, though. Instead, he asked Alice to continue to explain what happened next.

"I went outside to see what all the commotion was about. I tried to hang back in the crowd so that no one could see me, because I still felt self-conscious. But then, I heard someone accusing me of killing Trevor. They were yelling something about how I had fought with him earlier that evening, and how he had been trying to shut down my café. They said that made it obvious that I wanted him gone. Everyone started looking around for me, and I freaked out. I pulled my scarf over my head in hopes that no one would see me, and made a beeline for my car. As soon as I got there, I fled the parking lot as quickly as I could."

"Yeah, and then you didn't stop when we tried to pull you over," the other officer in the room interrupted. Mitch glared at him, clearly not happy with the interruption. But Alice didn't try to deny the fact. She just hung her head in shame.

"I'm sorry. I was scared, and not thinking clearly. I pulled onto a back road and hid until the police had passed. Then, after I'd waited about thirty minutes and hadn't heard any more sirens, I drove back to the library to see if Izzy was there. I knew she could help me, because she's solved so many murder cases before."

Mitch looked up at me and raised an eyebrow, and I shrugged slightly again.

I knew he wasn't happy with me for getting involved in this, but I hadn't been *trying* to get involved. It wasn't my fault that Alice had come back to the library to find me, and Mitch should just be grateful that I'd brought his suspect in for him.

Mitch continued on asking Alice more questions about what she and Trevor had been fighting over. Alice clearly didn't want to talk about it, although when Mitch pushed her she did admit that Trevor had been threatening to shut down her café. After it seemed that Mitch had gotten Alice to discuss everything she was willing to discuss, he looked up at her and said, "One more question: the initial report from the coroner said that Trevor had a chipped front tooth. This must be recent, since every time I've seen him, I've never noticed this. Do you know anything about that?"

I watched as Alice's face visibly paled. But then, she shook her head side to side and pounded her fist on the table again. "I have no idea why his tooth would be chipped. Why in the world would I know that? What are you trying to imply?"

Mitch sighed, clearly weary with this whole investigation already. "I'm not trying to imply anything. I'm just telling you what the coroner said and asking if you know anything about it. We're trying to figure out if it was a pre-existing injury, or whether it perhaps happened during the drowning."

I noticed he didn't say murder, but he also didn't say accident.

I thought Mitch was going to continue asking Alice questions about this, but instead, he stood and looked directly at me. "Izzy? A word, if you will?" Then he looked at Alice. "You can wait here with Officer Smith. Would you like some coffee or water or anything else to drink?"

Alice shook her head, so Mitch motioned to me to follow him. He led me to his office, where I'd been dozens of times before. Usually, when I was talking to him in here it was because he was fed up with my sticking my nose into one of his cases. Tonight was looking to be no different. As he sat behind his desk and I sat on the edge of the guest chair in his office, he gave me an exasperated look.

"Want to tell me what you're doing getting involved in all of this?"

"I had no choice," I insisted. "Alice showed up at the library begging for my help. She's my friend, and she feels alone and like no one's going to believe her. But I believe her, and because of that I'm going to help her. I just can't fathom the idea that she would actually kill someone."

I paused, expecting Mitch to agree with me. But he merely stared back at me with a pained expression on his face.

"What?" I demanded. "Don't tell me you actually think she committed the murder?"

Mitch sighed and cracked his knuckles. Then he ran his fingers through his hair, and cracked his knuckles again. It took a long time for him to actually speak.

"I have a hard time believing that Alice could commit a murder. But I have to tell you, it doesn't look good for her. We'll have to wait for a full, official autopsy before we can make any concrete determinations, but the initial reports I'm getting are that there was quite a great deal of trauma to Trevor's head. It looks like there was definitely a struggle. He had scratch marks on his neck and bruises on his back in addition to swelling on his head that was consistent with being struck by a blunt object."

I felt my stomach turn. "So it wasn't an accident. Someone pushed him in."

Mitch nodded and cracked his knuckles again. "I shouldn't be telling you this, but I know you'll find out soon enough, anyway. It definitely wasn't an accident. And, unfortunately, Alice was seen fighting with him quite dramatically less than an hour before the time of death. Again, we'll have to wait for the official autopsy to say for sure, but it looks like your friend is in hot water."

"*My* friend?" I choked out. "Isn't she your friend, too?"

Mitch dropped his gaze for a moment, then looked back up at me. I was surprised to see that his eyes looked like they were glistening with tears. He blinked quickly, and I thought for a moment that perhaps I had imagined it. But when he spoke, the emotion in his voice was unmistakable. "Of course she's my friend. But what am I supposed to do, Izzy? I'm the sheriff here, and I'm responsible for investigating situations like this. I can't let my personal relationships cloud my judgment. And you have to admit that any unbiased, outside observer would consider Alice to be a prime suspect."

"What about Norman?" I asked. "Wasn't he also fighting with Trevor? I heard that they'd been seen going at it in Alice's café a few days ago. And Trevor had been challenging Norman for the mayor's office. Surely, Norman had motive, too."

Mitch nodded wearily. "Norman is a person of interest as well. He was in here earlier and gave a statement. But despite the fact that he was fighting with Trevor, and was also the one who found the body, things just don't add up for him to be the criminal. Several people from the party remember talking to him minutes before he would have had to have killed Trevor. It's not absolutely impossible, but it would be difficult for the timing to add up. It would have had to have been an extremely fast attack and drowning for Norman to have been the one to do it."

I considered this information. From what Mitch was saying, it indeed did not sound good for Alice. But I still couldn't bring myself to believe that she was guilty. No matter how much she'd been fighting with Trevor, and no matter how innocent Norman might be, I couldn't process the idea that Alice had done this.

Still, I understood what Mitch was saying. He was the sheriff, and he had an official duty to follow all leads. There was no denying that Alice was objectively the most promising lead at the moment.

I tried to stay calm as I spoke to Mitch. "So what will you do? Will you arrest Alice?"

"No. At least, not yet," Mitch said. "The official autopsy hasn't come back saying it was foul play, so I won't take any action against her at this moment."

I nodded at him, grateful that he was at least waiting until things were official. I knew that that was the biggest concession he could make right now.

Mitch confirmed that fact for me when he continued on to say, "But it's coming. You know that, right? Once I get the official report that Trevor's death was not an accident, I'll be forced to charge Alice, assuming that between now and then no evidence comes up proving that she didn't do it. Right now, it looks too much like she committed the murder for me to ignore the evidence."

I nodded. "I understand. But you'll let her go for tonight, at least?"

"I'll let her go for tonight. And even if I have to charge her, I don't consider her a flight risk, so I'm happy to let her out on bail. But I know things won't be easy for her. She's going to feel even more humiliated once the whole town knows she's been charged with murder."

"Yeah. I know from experience just how fun it is to be a suspect in a murder case."

Mitch smiled sadly at me. He and I were both thinking of the murder case I'd gotten tangled up in when I first moved to Sunshine Springs. I'd been accused of poisoning someone with pie from my café. Of course, I'd eventually been proven innocent, but in the meantime things had been quite stressful.

"I don't suppose I can convince you to stay out of things?" Mitch asked.

I shrugged and shook my head at him. "No, sorry. Alice came to me as a friend, begging for my help. I can't turn her away."

Mitch nodded in resignation. By this point in our friendship, he knew that no matter how much he asked me to stay out of the case, if I wanted to be a part of it, nothing was going to stop me—especially not his pleas.

"Fine. But try to stay out of my way as much as possible. And don't go getting yourself in trouble."

I shrugged and grinned at him. "I'll try my best. But no promises. You know how crazy things get in these cases."

He groaned. "I know. Which is why I wish you would leave things well enough alone. But since you're determined not to, can I at least ask you to drive Alice home?"

"Of course," I said. "I'm sure she'll love the chance to discuss what just happened here at the station."

But as I drove away with Alice about fifteen minutes later, she wasn't in the mood to talk. The only thing she said was that she would rather I took her to her car so she could drive herself home, even though I offered to just take her straight home and come pick her up early the next day to get her car. She said she didn't want to be an inconvenience in the morning, and that she was determined to be at her café early to make sure that she opened on time and went about business as usual.

After explaining that, Alice was mostly silent. When I said goodbye, she thanked me again for my help, and begged me to continue looking into the case. But that was it.

I sat in the library parking lot for a few moments and watched her drive away. I had a feeling this wasn't going to be an easy case to crack, but for Alice's sake, I was determined to crack it. I'd start working on things the very next day in hopes that I would quickly find evidence to prove that Alice was innocent.

She was innocent, wasn't she? She had to be. There was just no world in which Alice Warner would have committed murder.

And yet, despite my reassurances to myself, I couldn't keep from replaying Mitch's pained words over and over in my head. He'd told me that things didn't look good for her, and I'd discovered many times before that people weren't who I thought they were at all.

Was I about to find out that Alice wasn't as innocent as she seemed? I gulped back my uneasy thoughts as I drove off into the darkness.

CHAPTER SEVEN

The next day, the mood around Sunshine Springs felt somber. Most of the town had been at the library's event that had ended in Trevor's death, and those who hadn't were quickly brought up to speed on what had happened.

Even though no official information had been released yet saying that the drowning was a murder and not an accident, everyone around town knew that it was just a matter of time. People whispered in my café, over glasses of wine and slices of boozy pie, discussing whether it was possible that Alice Warner had actually killed Trevor Truman. Some people held firmly to their belief that there was no possible way that Alice could have done something like that, while others almost gleefully said that they always knew she was a little bit too sweet.

"No one is actually as nice as Alice pretends to be," I heard more than one person say. "Poor old Trevor just finally pushed her buttons the wrong way and pushed her over the edge."

I tried to ignore the chatter and gossip as best I could. I did keep an ear open in case I heard anything interesting, but I didn't want anyone to ask me my opinion. I also didn't want to tell anyone that I was working on the case. I knew that once word got out that I was doing detective work once again, that no one was going to leave me alone about it. In my experience, when people knew I was working on a case, I couldn't take an order for pie at the Drunken Pie Café without being expected to give a complete rundown on everything I'd learned on the case.

Right now, I definitely wasn't in the mood to be giving any rundowns. I'd texted Alice early in the day to ask her how she was doing, and to let her know that I was around if she needed me. She'd texted me back to thank me and say that she was hanging in there. She said she was at her café, and trying to go about business as usual.

I had no doubt that her café would be extremely busy today. The majority of people in Sunshine Springs would be stopping by there to see if they could get her to make any sort of comment on the case. I hoped that for her sake she would stay away from the front counter today and make her other employees do most of the work that involved speaking directly with customers.

Thankfully for me, I also had an employee to help me out now. Even before Trevor's drowning had taken place, Tiffany had been scheduled to work the closing shift at the Drunken Pie Café for the day after the library's party. That meant that I was able to escape my pie shop in the early afternoon and head off to do some detective work.

I took Sprinkles along with me, which I didn't often do when I was sleuthing. He wasn't allowed inside most buildings, and he usually preferred to hang out with Grams because of that. He didn't like waiting outside, and I couldn't blame him.

But today, I wanted to keep him close. I had an uneasy feeling about chasing down a murderer. I was more careful these days than I had been in my early detective days. Now, after having had my own life threatened a few times by criminals, I knew that there was some truth to what Mitch said: these cases could be awfully dangerous, and while Sprinkles wasn't exactly what you'd call a guard dog, he was still fiercely protective of me. Having him close by eased my nerves somewhat.

He rode along with me as I drove down to the government district of Sunshine Springs. The "district" consisted of a few small government buildings on the edge of downtown. This was where the offices for the elections committee were located—including the office of Sydney Joyner. I decided that talking to her might be a good place to start. Since she knew all of the election candidates, maybe she could tell me something about who else might have been fighting with Trevor. Or perhaps she could shed some light on whether Norman had actually been fighting with Trevor severely enough to make it a real possibility that Norman might have been the one to drown Trevor.

But to my dismay, Sydney was nowhere to be found. A sign hanging on her office door simply stated that she was out for the day. When I asked someone in an office a few doors down, they laughed, as though asking where Sydney was must have been some sort of joke.

"Sydney? She didn't come in today. I don't think she'll be coming in tomorrow, either. From what I understand, she's on the verge of a nervous breakdown over what happened with Trevor. As if she wasn't already stressed enough with everything surrounding the mayor's election, now she's found herself at the center of a drowning scandal."

I frowned. "Why is she at the center? I know she works in the elections office, but is it really fair to say she was at the center of all this, especially when Alice is apparently the prime suspect? Alice doesn't have much to do with the elections office, does she?"

The girl paled slightly, but then shrugged. "I just meant that the death of one candidate for mayor while another candidate for mayor is a suspected murderer in that death means that Sydney's life has been suddenly filled with quite a bit of drama. She can't avoid questions when she'd worked with both Norman and Trevor in the last few months. Sydney's not one to enjoy being involved in drama, and this is quite a bit of drama, wouldn't you agree?"

I frowned. Something about the way this girl was talking about things made me think that there was more to Sydney's absence than just the fact that she didn't like drama. I couldn't be sure, but it seemed to me that this girl was darting her eyes around a little too quickly even as she refused to make eye contact with me. She was hiding something, but what? Did Sydney know something about this case that this girl also knew?

I narrowed my eyes at the girl, trying to look stern. But the effect was lost on her, since she still refused to meet my gaze.

"When might I expect Sydney to be back in the office?" I finally asked.

The girl shrugged, still staring anywhere but at my face. "Beats me. I'd say she's probably going to stay away for a few days, at least."

The girl went back to typing something in her computer, a clear hint that it was time for me to leave, and that she wasn't going to discuss the matter further.

I decided I was wasting my time here, and walked away without another word. But I felt I had learned at least one thing: Sydney might know something, and she might be more involved in this case than anyone had suspected. I would have to find a way to track her down around town. Just because she wasn't coming in to work didn't mean that I wouldn't be able to talk to her.

But even though this trip hadn't been completely useless, I couldn't help feeling a bit dejected as I headed toward the building's exit. If I didn't find information to clear Alice's name soon, she was going to be officially charged. I knew that would devastate her, but with every second that passed, I knew it was going to be harder and harder to avoid. I would just have to do my best to explain to Alice that Mitch had no choice in the matter, and that I would continue working hard to clear her name.

I had almost reached the building's exit when I remembered that Cody Stringer's office was in this building as well. I remembered hearing him brag a few months ago about how he'd been able to move his office here thanks to the notoriety that working on Trevor's campaign had brought him. Perhaps it was worth paying Cody a visit. I knew from his ranting last night that he considered Norman the top suspect. Would he still feel that way today, after more information had come out? Would he perhaps have any more detailed information to give me on the feud between Norman and

Trevor? Or maybe he even knew why Trevor had been so determined to shut down Alice's café. He was perhaps even closer to this case than Sydney was, and I would be remiss if I didn't pay him a visit.

I found a building directory and quickly located Cody's office number. He was on the second floor, and I took the stairs up two at a time toward his office. But when I reached the office, I was disappointed to find a "Closed" sign on the door. The front of the office contained frosted glass windows and a door of frosted glass, so I could see that the inside of the office was dark as well. Either Cody hadn't come in today, or he'd left already.

I shouldn't have been surprised by this. If Sydney hadn't come in due to being too connected to the case, then of course Cody hadn't. As Trevor's campaign manager, he was closer to Trevor and knew the man better than anyone in Sunshine Springs. Feeling even more dejected, I sighed and turned to go.

But just as I turned, a flash of movement caught my eye from inside the office. At first, I thought I'd imagined it. But just to be sure, I paused for a moment to stare intently at the frosted glass wall of the office. Sure enough, a moment later I saw the unmistakable flash of a shadow moving across the office.

My pulse quickened as I watched the shadow moving back and forth. With the thickness of the frosted glass, it was impossible to see who the shadow belonged to, but one thing I knew for sure: the person definitely wasn't Cody. Whoever was sneaking around in there wasn't nearly skinny enough to be Cody "string bean" Stringer.

My heart started to pound in my chest, and I wondered whether Cody knew that this person was in his office. My guess was probably not. If someone was supposed to be in there, why would they have all the lights off and the door sign set to "Closed?" This person was sneaking around looking for something, but what? Was it something related to Trevor and his murder?

The shadow started moving toward the office's front door, and I panicked. If this was the murderer, I didn't want them to know I was watching them. I looked around frantically but I didn't have time to run. The hallway was too long, and if the intruder came out now they might see me running away. If they recognized me, then I was in trouble.

In the midst of my panic, I noticed a giant fake tree that I might be able to hide behind if I stood in exactly the right spot and remained perfectly still. It was worth a shot. I ran over and threw myself behind it just as the door to Cody's office clicked open.

I prayed that I wouldn't be seen, and held my breath as the intruder slowly closed the door and then locked it with a key. I let my breath out a little bit. If this person had a key, then perhaps they weren't an intruder after all. Maybe they had just needed to quickly get something for Cody and hadn't bothered to turn on the lights.

I chanced a peek through the leaves of the tree, and had to stifle back a gasp at what I saw. Ambling down the hallway away from Cody's office, with a giant stack of green folders and papers in his arms, I saw Norman Wade.

What in the world was Norman doing in Cody's office? Cody had been working as the campaign manager for Trevor—Norman's opponent—so there would have been no reason for Cody and Norman to be working together. There definitely wouldn't have been a reason for Norman to have a key to Cody's office.

Norman paused, and turned to look behind him as though he had heard something. I held my breath again, terrified that he was going to see me there. But his eyes glazed right over the tree, and he didn't seem to notice that there was a person pressed behind it.

I, however, noticed how tired his face looked. He had dark circles under his eyes, and I wondered if he'd slept at all the night before. His expression looked wary and frightened, exactly the way you'd expect someone's face to look if they'd been sneaking around in an office where they didn't belong.

After a moment of looking down the hallway, Norman turned back around and quickly walked away. I remained frozen behind the tree for several minutes after he left, worried that he was going to reappear around the corner at any moment. When nothing moved in the hallway for several minutes, I decided to make a break for it.

I quickly ran down the hallway and down the stairs, then rushed outside where I found Sprinkles waiting for me. I looked around, half-expecting to see Norman standing there angrily accusing me of spying on him. But other than Sprinkles, no one was out on the sidewalk right then. I wasn't sure whether to be happy or disappointed about that. Had Norman come out this exit? And where was he going with all those papers he had taken? What were all of those papers he had taken?

Just as I was about to give up and head back to my car, I saw a flash of movement to my left. Norman was coming around the corner of the building and heading straight toward me. Luckily, he was staring down at the pile of papers that he still held, so he didn't notice me. Quickly, I jumped behind some bushes, pulling Sprinkles with me. Thankfully, Sprinkles seemed to sense that this was not the time to start whining or barking. He remained as still as I did, and Norman walked right by the two of us without ever seeing us.

Once Norman was a safe distance away, I decided that I needed to follow him. He was up to something, and I had a strong feeling that whatever that something was, it wasn't good. I also had a feeling that it was related to Trevor's murder, and that Norman was more involved in all of this than he'd led me to believe.

"Come on, Sprinkles," I whispered. "Let's see where this fool is going. Perhaps we'll have solved this case before Mitch has to arrest Alice, after all."

CHAPTER EIGHT

Norman walked at a quick pace, looking around every so often as though nervous that someone might be watching him. Every time he turned back, I managed to quickly jump behind a tree or bush with Sprinkles. As far as I could tell, he never noticed that I was watching him, but the stress of following him like that was making my heart feel like it was going to pound right out of my chest.

Thankfully, Norman wasn't going very far. He headed straight for a building half a block down that housed more government offices, including the mayor's office. I figured he was taking all of those green folders he'd swiped from Cody back to his own office. I glanced at my watch. It was nearly five o'clock, so many of the city employees would be heading home. Had Norman purposefully timed things this way so that he wouldn't be bothered by too many people and could review these papers alone in his office?

Whatever his intentions were, I was sure they weren't good.

I once again left Sprinkles outside, and he dejectedly flopped down on a grassy spot beneath a tree. I wished more than anything that I could have brought him in with me, but strolling through City Hall with a Dalmatian trailing me was bound to draw attention. The last thing I wanted to do right now was draw attention to myself.

I continued following Norman slowly, keeping a safe distance so he wouldn't notice me. I wasn't sure what to do next. Should I call Mitch and tell him what I'd seen, leaving it to him to come in here and question Norman about the papers? Or should I just confront him myself directly? But what would I say?

I saw you in Cody's office. Now hand over what you've got.

I couldn't force him to do that, and he might deny that he had any papers. Or, if he was the murderer, he might get angry and try to hurt me.

Even though I hated to ask for help, I decided it might be better to have Mitch come look at things. At the very least, perhaps I should come back later when Norman wasn't around, and see if I could get any information from his secretary. She might know of some reason why Norman was taking papers from Cody's office. Maybe this whole thing was benign.

But then, I almost laughed at that thought. I didn't see how it could possibly be benign. This all screamed of scandal, and I had a strong feeling that the papers were related to Trevor's murder. I didn't want to talk to Norman's secretary while he was around, though. He was bound to be upset if he knew I was poking around in his business, especially if he was indeed guilty.

With my mind made up that I would come back later, I turned to go. But just then, Norman's secretary walked out into the hallway. She was a regular at my café, and although I didn't know her well personally, I did recognize her—and I could have told you her exact pie order: strawberry moonshine pie, with a no foam latte if it was before three P.M., or a glass of Pinot if it was after 3 P.M.

Her face lit up when she saw me. "Izzy! Good to see you. What are you doing here? Did you need to see Norman? He's still in, although he might be about to leave." She glanced at her watch. "It's almost five, and I was about to take off. But if you'd like, I can let him know you're here."

For a moment, I froze. What was I supposed to say? If I didn't come up with a good reason for being here, she might get suspicious of me. Then she was bound to mention to Norman that I had stopped by, which would make him suspicious of me. If he was the murderer, he would probably know that I was onto him. Not only would I lose any element of surprise that I might have, but I would also have put myself on a murderer's list of people to dislike. That didn't sound like the best option, so I had to come up with an excuse, and fast.

I gave her a sugary sweet smile. "Would you mind letting him know I'm here? I understand if he's busy. I'm sure it's been a rough day for him. But I wanted to swing by and check on him if possible. You may have heard that I was the one he originally came to when he found Trevor drowned in the fountain, so I saw firsthand just how upset the mayor was. I wanted to check in on him and see how he was holding up."

Norman's secretary patted my arm and shook her head at me sadly. "You are just the sweetest thing, Izzy. I'm sure you yourself have had quite a time of it, so it just shows what a caring person you are that you thought to take the time to come check on the mayor. I'll go see if he's available to chat for a moment. I'm sure he'll be happy to see you."

I'm not so sure about that, I thought as I followed her back into the reception area outside the mayor's office. I sat down on an overstuffed couch while she went in to let him know I was there. I felt guilty that she thought that I was such a sweet, caring person. She would probably be horrified if she knew that the real reason I was there was that I suspected her boss of murder.

Then again, I shouldn't feel too badly. If Norman had committed murder, then he deserved to be spied on.

A few moments later, his secretary came out and waved me in. "He said to go right in. I'm taking off, so I won't see you again when you leave. But thank you for stopping by. Hopefully I'll see you around the café this week. After the time we've all had, I'll definitely be needing some pie." She winked at me, and I tried to muster up a smile as I turned to head into the mayor's office.

I gulped back my fear as I knocked on the door frame of the open door to announce my arrival. The mayor was looking down at a stack of papers, and didn't bother to look up at me.

"Come in and sit down."

He didn't say that he was happy to see me, and he definitely didn't sound like he was. I tried to see what papers he was looking at without being obvious about it, but whatever it was looked like some sort of boring city contracts. I did notice a large stack of green folders sitting on one of the bookshelves in his office—a stack that looked exactly like the set of folders I'd seen him sneaking out of Cody's office. I wished more than anything that I could jump up, grab the folders, and run.

But that would be a ridiculous thing to do. I was sure Norman would chase after me with gusto, and even if he didn't catch me, he'd probably do everything he could to make sure I didn't get those papers to Mitch. If he'd killed Trevor, he'd probably be willing to kill someone else to keep his name clear.

On the other hand, if those papers turned out to be something completely mundane, then I'd look ridiculous running off with them. No, the best thing to do right now was to bide my time and act like I really was just here to check in on him.

I smiled sweetly at him, just as I had at his secretary a few minutes earlier. "How are you holding up, Mr. Mayor? I was worried about you after everything that happened last night. I just wanted to stop by and make sure you're doing okay."

But Norman did not react at all like his secretary had. Instead, he looked up at me with an angry scowl on his face. "Oh, cut the crap, Izzy."

I gulped, but tried to act like I didn't know what he was talking about. "Whatever do you mean?" I asked, trying to sound as innocent as possible.

Even as I spoke the words, I felt a sick fear rising within me. Had I been wrong to think that I'd gotten away with sneaking after him when he left Cody's office? Had he actually seen me?

It took every ounce of self-control in my body to keep from jumping up and running out of that office. But if I did that, then I was admitting that there was truth to his accusing glare. So instead of running, I sat as still as I possibly could and tried to look like I genuinely had no idea what he was talking about.

He snorted at me derisively. "Don't act so innocent. I know why you're here. I know you're not really checking up on me. You're actually trying to spy on me. Admit it."

I gulped again, but there was no way I was actually admitting that. "Spy on you?" I said in a shocked tone of voice. "Why in the world would I spy on you? I just wanted to see how you're doing after last night."

Norman snorted at me again. "You wanted to see how I was doing, or you wanted to see whether there was any truth to the police's suspicions of me?"

"I… I…" I wasn't sure what to say. As I fumbled over my words, trying to come up with the best way to deny his accusations, he slammed his fist down on the table. I jumped with a small shriek.

"Yeah, you'd better be scared. I'm a powerful man in this city. You know that, right? If you think you can run around spying on me and trying to pin this murder on me, then you're an even bigger fool than I thought."

"I'm not trying to pin any murder on you!" I insisted.

In reality, I was beginning to think that he was looking guiltier by the second. But he clearly wasn't scared of me. He leaned back in his chair and crossed his arms.

"I know that you're working on this murder case."

I must have looked surprised, because he quickly added, "Don't look so shocked. Did you really think you could hide the fact that you're trying to play detective again? Everyone in town is talking about how you're running around trying to prove Alice's innocence. To be honest, I don't know why Mitch puts up with you. If I were him, I'd have you arrested for interfering with criminal investigations. But I guess he has a soft spot for you and thinks that one of these days you're actually going to date him."

"Mitch and I are good friends. What he does or doesn't put up with from me has nothing to do with him thinking I might date him."

I felt hot anger rising within me and heating my cheeks. To be honest, I wasn't exactly sure how true my words were. Mitch *did* want to date me. Was that really the reason he put up with me? I liked to think that our friendship had a sound basis beyond just any potential romantic interest Mitch might have held. But was that really the case? Was I a fool to think that he did care about me as a person, regardless of whether he and I ever had a relationship?

I didn't have much time to ponder those questions right then, and I didn't know whether to be more or less convinced that Norman was guilty by the fact that he was so angry at me for investigating the case. I felt immensely annoyed that it had already gotten out that I was attempting to solve this case. Who had figured that out and spread the gossip? Surely, Alice hadn't?

Or maybe she had. Maybe she thought if she put out the word that I was on the case, that it would put pressure on the real murderer and would make him think that he was going to be found out soon.

No doubt, Norman had noticed my discomfort. He sneered at me.

"I see you don't deny any of this. Well, at least you're not trying to lie to me. But don't think that means I'm going to forgive you for sneaking around after me. I didn't murder Trevor, so you're wasting your time trying to prove that I did. You might as well accept now that your friend Alice is guilty. The evidence is all there. It's so obvious. No one in town wants to believe that the sweet owner of the Morning Brew Café finally snapped, but she did. Open your eyes, Izzy. This is an open and shut case. And now, I'd appreciate it if you'd open and shut the door to my office and get out of here."

I decided that the best thing to do was to leave as he was asking. With one last, longing glance at the green folders piled on his bookshelf, I stood and turned to leave. I was dying with curiosity to know what was in those folders, but there was no way I was going to find out right now.

As I left Norman's office, however, I had already moved him to the top of my suspect list, and I was already trying to figure out the best way to get my hands on those folders.

I felt pretty confident that whatever was in them was something that would incriminate him. He could accuse Alice all he wanted, but I wasn't buying those angry accusations. I *did* have my eyes open, and I could see what was right in front of me. Norman was the one hiding something here. I was going to figure out what it was he was hiding, and how it related to Trevor's murder.

I just hoped that I figured it out before Norman figured out a way to shut me up for good. I could tell from the look on his face that he would have loved nothing more than to do just that.

Trying to squelch the panic rising within me, I rushed out of the building without another look back. I had some serious work to do.

CHAPTER NINE

After leaving the government office building, I decided to head over to the Morning Brew Café and see if I could catch Alice. It was already past closing time for her café, but I knew she often stayed late to get a head start on prepping the café for the next day. Perhaps she would still be around.

If she was, I was going to ask her if she'd been speaking to anyone about Trevor's murder case. And if she had been, I was going to advise her to stop. Spreading more rumors wasn't going to help, and having people following me around wondering if I really was investigating the case would only slow down my efforts.

Not that I could stop everyone in town from gossiping about my detective efforts now. It was clearly a bit too late for that. News traveled fast in Sunshine Springs, and with everyone focused on the fact that Trevor had died the night before, any news about the case was bound to quickly make the rounds. Still, I figured it was worth a try to ask Alice to lay off on discussing the case.

When I got to the Morning Brew Café, everything was quiet. Alice was nowhere to be seen, and the inside of the café was completely dark. She must have gone home early for the day instead of sticking around to prep things for tomorrow. I couldn't blame her. I knew it wouldn't take long for the gossip about the case to get out of control, and I was sure that Alice didn't want to be surrounded by people asking her questions about it.

I hadn't heard anything yet about an official report from the coroner, but I had a feeling that the report would come sometime within the next twenty-four hours. After that, Mitch would be forced to arrest Alice. I desperately wanted to solve the case before then, but I knew that it wasn't realistic to think that was possible. The best I could do would be to prepare Alice for the inevitability that she was going to be an official murder suspect, but to try to make her feel less scared by that possibility.

I figured I'd try to find Alice at her home since she wasn't at the café. But as I was leaving, I noticed someone sneaking around the outside of the café, peeking in the front window. I went to investigate, and was surprised to see that it was Sydney Joyner. Before I could think about what I was doing, I confronted her.

"Sydney? What are you doing here?"

Sydney turned to look at me, and to my surprise I saw her sneer at me. Maybe I shouldn't have been surprised, since so far nobody seemed happy with the idea that I was going to be working on this case. But I didn't see what reason Sydney would have to dislike me. I knew she was upset by Trevor's death. But it's not like it was my fault he had died. I was trying to bring him justice, even though my motivation behind doing that was to help Alice and not necessarily because I had cared that much about Trevor. But still, the end effect would be that Trevor would get justice. Shouldn't Sydney be happy about that?

But Sydney was anything but happy. She scowled at me and made no attempt to hide the fact that she was not pleased to see me.

"What are you doing here?" she countered. "No, wait, don't answer that. I already know: You're here to talk to Alice to figure out how you can get her off the hook and to try to frame Norman for Trevor's drowning. Really, Izzy. I'm disappointed in you. I know that Alice is your friend, but surely you can see that she's the guilty one here."

I paused and bit my lower lip to keep myself from retorting in anger. I should have known. Of course that's why Sydney wasn't happy to see me. She didn't see me as getting justice for Trevor, she saw me as trying to cause problems for the remaining candidate for mayor. From what I understood, she'd been close to both Trevor and Norman. Now that she'd lost Trevor, she must have been twice as determined not to lose Norman, too.

I could see how my working on this case would be a threat to her, because no matter how you looked at things, there was evidence that made Norman look guilty. Yes, you could look at the evidence and think that Alice was guilty, too. I wouldn't deny that. Personally, of course, I didn't believe Alice was guilty. But I could see how people would think that. The same could be said for Norman, though. If Sydney was going to claim that one couldn't overlook the evidence for Alice, then surely she had to admit that the same could be said for Norman.

But Sydney didn't look like she was exactly in the mood to be rational about all of this. She looked like she was in the mood to fight with me, but I wasn't interested in arguing with her. I tried to keep my tone of voice neutral as I spoke to her.

"Look, I'm not going to deny that I took on this case to try to help Alice. I do believe that she's innocent, but I can acknowledge that there is some evidence against her. But surely, you can also acknowledge that there is some evidence against Norman. I'm just trying to get to the bottom of what all of the evidence points to."

But Sydney would not be reasoned with. She glared at me, and lowered her voice to a furious, seething tone. "All of the evidence points to Alice. You saw how she fought with Trevor, and you know he was trying to shut down her café. Not to mention, she was missing for the whole timeframe during which Trevor drowned. Sure, she says she was in the bathroom. But no one saw her there. Meanwhile, plenty of people saw Norman right around the time of the drowning."

"Yes, right around the time," I countered. "But there was a portion of time that he can't find a witness to account for him. It's possible that the drowning occurred during that time, which means it's possible Norman was the murderer. And he had motive, too. Everyone knows that Norman was worried that Trevor was actually going to steal the mayor's office away from him. From what I've heard, the two of them fought quite a bit as well."

But Sydney was not convinced. She shook her head at me as though I was the world's most gullible person. Part of me wondered if I was. Was I defending Alice when she didn't deserve it?

I mentally chided myself. No. There was just no way that Alice was guilty of this. I frowned at Sydney and crossed my arms. "You know as well as I do that Alice has been a pillar in the community for a long time. Norman might be the mayor, but he has a streak of politician in him. You can't deny that. I'm pretty sure that he was looking out for his own interests much more than Alice was looking out for hers. If anyone felt threatened by Trevor enough to kill him, my money is on the man who was about to lose the position of mayor to Trevor. It just adds up better. There's not any more evidence against Alice than there is against Norman, and sneaking around the café like this isn't going to turn up anything more."

Sydney snorted. "Oh, trust me. There's a lot more evidence against Alice than there is against Norman."

I raised an eyebrow at her. "How so?"

Sydney tossed her curly red hair over her shoulder. "Why don't you ask Alice to tell you about Trevor's chipped tooth? That might be a good place to start."

My frown deepened. "Chipped tooth?" I asked, dumbly. Why was that ringing a bell?

Then I remembered that Mitch had mentioned something about that the night before. He'd asked Alice if she knew anything about the chipped tooth, and Alice had gotten quite defensive over it. I'd just figured that Alice was getting defensive over everything because she was so upset about being under suspicion. But what if there was more to it than that. Why was Sydney bringing this up, and how did she know about the chipped tooth?

I tried to remain calm as I spoke. "Mitch already told me about the chipped tooth. That's not news. It just shows that there must have been a struggle when Trevor was thrown into the fountain. Honestly, that points to Norman more than to Alice. Alice would have had a hard time throwing a man as big as Trevor into the water, so it must have been someone more powerful, like Norman."

I gave Sydney a triumphant look, as though that settled things. But Sydney laughed at me.

"That chipped tooth wasn't from any sort of struggle around the fountain. You know as well as I do that Trevor was drunk enough that practically anyone could have forced him into the fountain, even an old grandma. But that's beside the point, because that chipped tooth wasn't the sign of a struggle around the fountain. That chipped tooth happened days before, in Alice's café."

This was news to me, and even though I tried to hide my surprise, Sydney must have seen the shock on my face. She got a triumphant look on her own face as she continued to speak.

"Oh, your little friend Alice didn't tell you about that?" She leaned in to get right in my face. "Well, maybe you should ask her. I'm sure she won't be happy to know that you found out. Trust me: you might have a different view of this murder case after she's forced to come clean with you about that chipped tooth."

"Even if the chipped tooth did happen days earlier at Alice's café, what does that have to do with the murder?" I said, keeping my arms crossed and doing my best to keep the fear from rising in my face.

But Sydney must have known that she had me. She didn't answer other than to smirk at me. Then she walked past me, purposely bumping my shoulder as she did.

I turned to watch her go, unsure of how I should feel about all of this. I'd never thought that Sydney was a mean person, but she certainly wasn't acting very nice right now. Did she have a legitimate reason for acting so snotty about Alice? What would I find out if I did ask Alice about the chipped tooth?

There was only one way to find out. As much as I hated to take Sydney's advice, I knew that I had to follow this lead and see what was behind this whole chipped tooth business.

I glanced down at Sprinkles, who was watching me with a worried expression on his face.

"Come on, buddy. I guess it's time to pay a visit to Alice at her house. We need to find out what Sydney is talking about, and something tells me this is too urgent of a matter to wait until the next time I happen to run into Alice."

Sprinkles growled at Sydney's receding form, but then followed me as I climbed back into my car and started driving toward Alice's house. I didn't want to think too hard about what I might find when I questioned her, but it was hard not to let my mind jump to some disturbing conclusions.

CHAPTER TEN

I half-expected that I wouldn't even find Alice at her house. She'd been so skittish that I thought perhaps she would have tried to hide out somewhere that no one would look for her. But when I arrived, she opened the door for me before I even had a chance to ring the doorbell. She must have been watching her front yard from her kitchen window when I drove up.

"Izzy!" she exclaimed as she threw open the front door. "Thank goodness you're here. Did you figure out who murdered Trevor?"

She looked so hopeful that it broke my heart a little to have to tell her that I had not yet cracked the case. As I shook my head no, I watched her face fall. She blinked a few times as though trying to blink away tears, and wiped her hands on her apron as though trying to wipe away the worries that were consuming her.

"I suppose that would have been too much to hope for," she said sadly. "I'm just so stressed out about all of this. Please, come in. Feel free to bring Sprinkles in as well. I'm just making some batches of chocolate."

I'd figured she was baking, since she was wearing her apron. But I was surprised when I followed her into her kitchen at just how big of an operation she had going on in there. Every square inch of her kitchen counters was covered with ingredients, mixing bowls, or other baking paraphernalia. Sprinkles' eyes widened as well, and I gave him a stern look to warn him not to try to swipe any chocolate. He knew chocolate was off-limits and would make him sick, but that didn't necessarily mean he wouldn't attempt to grab some.

Meanwhile, Alice actually managed a small laugh when she saw me taking it all in.

"It's a lot, isn't it? I could do all of this down at the café, but I don't want to spend my entire life there. It's nice to be home and work on this from here a little bit. Of course, Trevor thought that was unacceptable. He was trying to shut down my whole café just because I was making all of this chocolate here instead of down the road at the café. The whole thing was so ridiculous. But now I wish I had never fought with him. It's being used as ammunition to try to make it look like I killed him."

Alice's voice quavered at this last part, and I couldn't detect any note of fakeness in her voice. Either she really hadn't killed Trevor, or she was an incredible actress. She definitely did not seem like someone who felt guilty for taking the life of another human being. Still, I had to figure out what the deal was with the chipped tooth. If Mitch and Sydney had both brought it up, then there must be more to that story than Alice had originally let on.

I took a deep breath, and dove into my questions. "I've been asking around about Trevor's murder, and I've been following up on a few leads. But while doing that, I learned some information about Trevor's chipped tooth. I heard that the tooth was actually chipped at your café a few days ago. Is that true?"

Alice looked up at me and her face paled. "No! That's not true at all! I have no idea how his tooth was chipped. I didn't even realize that it was chipped in the first place."

She crossed her arms dramatically, and I sighed. "Alice, you're a horrible liar."

Her face fell. "Is it that obvious that I knew about the tooth?"

"Yes. Your face gives everything away. Now, do you want to tell me the truth about that tooth?"

Alice buried her head in her hands for a moment, then looked up at me with a contrite expression on her face. "Whoever told you that Trevor chipped the tooth at my café was telling you the truth. Trevor had been coming around to harass me at my café quite a bit. I don't know why he was always in there if he hated me so much. I guess he liked to cause trouble for me. But anyway, one day last week when he was in there, he suddenly started howling in pain. Then he came up to the counter showing me a piece of his tooth that he'd chipped on a mug."

I frowned. "How did he manage to chip his tooth on a mug?"

Alice shrugged helplessly. "I have no idea. I've had that café for over a decade, and I've never had anyone chip their tooth on anything. But somehow, Trevor managed to do so. At least that's what he claimed. He came running up to the counter and yelled at me, telling me he was going to sue me for the chipped tooth. I apologized and told him that I didn't think I was at fault because there was nothing wrong with the mug. It's not my problem if a grown man doesn't know how to sip out of a mug without chipping his tooth!"

I couldn't help but laugh. "I agree with you on that."

Alice cracked a small smile, but then frowned. "Well, he clearly didn't agree. He threatened to sue, and I didn't know what to do so I told him he'd have to speak with my lawyer about that."

I raised an eyebrow. "You have a lawyer?" It hadn't sounded like she did when she was speaking with Mitch the other night, but perhaps she just meant she didn't have a criminal lawyer. She very well might have had a lawyer helping her with her business dealings.

But Alice was shaking her head. "I don't have a lawyer, but I suppose I would have needed to get one if Trevor had actually gone through with suing me. That's all a moot point now, though, since he's dead."

I winced. "Alice! It's not exactly a moot point. The fact that Trevor had been threatening to sue you could be seen as a motivation for you to murder him."

Alice looked at me blankly for a few moments, as though not understanding. Once again, I thought that she either was genuinely innocent and shocked by all of this, or she was one of the better actresses I'd ever encountered.

"I don't understand," she said.

I sighed. "You said it yourself: now that Trevor's dead, there's no threat of him suing you over his chipped tooth. A jury could look at that and think that you had murdered him to keep him from suing you. That's on top of the fact that he was trying to shut down your café for this homemade chocolate operation." I moved my hand in a sweeping gesture that encompassed the kitchen and all of the chocolate-making ingredients. "It's a bit worrisome how much easier your life is now that Trevor is gone."

Alice's eyes widened. "Well, I'm not going to lie: it has made my life quite a bit easier. But I didn't kill him. I would never take someone's life just to make my own life easier, even if that person was trying to destroy my entire livelihood."

I rubbed my forehead. "You should have told Mitch about all of this last night. And you should have told me, if you seriously want me to work on solving this case for you. If you hold information back, it's only going to make you look worse to Mitch, and make my job of proving your innocence that much harder."

Alice's eyes darkened with anger. "I just don't see how it's relevant that Trevor threatened to sue me. The whole thing was so ridiculous, and he wouldn't have won, anyway."

I shook my head at her. "Don't bury your head in the sand. You're on the verge of being charged with murder. All of these little details matter, and the way we handle them matters. I believe you when you say you're innocent. But to prove that innocence, I need to know what I'm up against. Can you please just promise that you'll be more open with me in the future?"

Alice shrugged in a noncommittal fashion. "I guess I'll try. But it just doesn't seem right to me that I have to worry about all these little details."

I wanted to reach across the kitchen counter and shake some sense into my friend. I understood that she must be upset and somewhat in denial about everything, but I wished she would understand how badly it looked for her when she hid potential evidence.

I stayed with Alice for about twenty more minutes, trying to ask her if she could think of anything else that she needed to tell me about Trevor and his dealings with the Morning Brew Café. But I wasn't sure she truly understood the gravity of the situation.

Finally, I gave up and decided to go home to try to sort through the clues I did have and decide what my next step should be. I bid Alice a quick goodbye and went with Sprinkles to my car. As I turned the car on, I decided to give Molly a call. It had been a while since I'd enlisted her help on a murder case, and I felt I could use someone to bounce ideas off of right now. Molly tended to be pretty good at seeing things a little differently than I did, and sometimes all I needed to unravel clues was somebody else's perspective on the situation. Maybe if I talked through everything on this case with her, then my next steps would become clear.

"Izzy!" Molly said excitedly into the phone after the first ring. "What are you up to?"

"Sleuthing," I said. "What are you up to? It's really noisy wherever you are."

"I'm at Sophia's. I decided it was time to get my hair done again. I want to look my best at all times in case Scott, well…you know."

I laughed into the phone. Despite the fact that Grams had made it clear that everyone in Sunshine Springs already knew that Scott was planning on proposing to Molly, Molly still didn't want to say anything about it out loud. And if she was trying to avoid being gossiped about, then she was right to keep quiet while she was at Sophia's Snips.

Sophia had a monopoly on the beauty market in Sunshine Springs. Her salon and spa was the only place in town to go to if you wanted a haircut, a facial, waxing, a massage, or to get your nails done. It was a one-stop beauty shop.

It was also a one-stop gossip shop. It was the best place to hear the latest town news. If anyone at Sophia's got the slightest hint that Molly thought Scott was proposing soon, then the news definitely would be all over town.

I smiled. "Well, assuming you don't have a date with Scott tonight, do you want to come over for some pie and wine? I'd love your take on a few things that have been happening in this case."

"I think that will work. Scott told me he has to work late tonight. He's behind on deliveries because he took so much time off to help me get ready for the fountain dedication yesterday. Personally, I think the real reason he's behind is that he took time off to go ring shopping. But obviously I can't question him about that."

Molly giggled, and I smiled. It was good to hear my friend in good spirits, even though things for the fountain dedication last night hadn't gone as she'd planned.

"Great," I said, feeling excited already at the prospect of seeing her. "I'm just going to run by the pie shop to see what pies I have leftover from today. I'll grab some pie and then I'll—"

"Wait!" Molly interrupted. "If you have any strawberry moonshine pie, can you bring that? I've been craving a piece."

I laughed. "Of course. I probably will have some left. I've been making quite a bit of it because I have extra strawberries right now, and—"

"Uh-oh," Molly suddenly interrupted me again. "Forget about the pie, Izzy."

"What?" I asked in confusion. "Why?"

"The pie can wait," Molly said, lowering her voice as though telling me a secret. "You better get down here."

"To Sophia's Snips? Why?"

"Trust me. Just get down here. You're gonna want to see this."

Molly hung up the phone without another word, and I glanced over at Sprinkles and shrugged. "I have no idea what's going on, but I guess we better go check it out. Molly wouldn't have told me to come down there like that if it wasn't something important."

Sprinkles barked enthusiastically, and I turned my car in the direction of Sophia's Snips, which thankfully was only a few minutes' drive away.

I hoped that whatever Molly was so excited about had something to do with Trevor's murder case. Was I about to get another clue? My heart beat faster at the possibility.

CHAPTER ELEVEN

When I pulled into the parking lot at Sophia's Snips, nothing looked out of the ordinary. The parking lot was full of cars, but that was nothing special. At any given time during business hours, there were likely to only be a few spots open in the parking lot here. I saw Grams' car, which also was not unusual. Grams was here several times a week, and usually she brought Sprinkles with her when she came. She liked to have the nail techs paint his nails, and I had long since given up on telling her that my boy Dalmatian didn't need nail polish. The only reason he wasn't already inside with Grams today was that I'd wanted him with me as I checked out clues in the murder case. Now that we were at the salon, though, he barked excitedly and wagged his tail. I let out a long sigh.

"Listen, Sprinkles. We're not here to get your nails painted."

He looked at me so forlornly that I had to laugh. "Okay, maybe if we have time you can get your nails painted. I'm sure since we're here, Grams is going to insist on it. But no promises. I don't know why Molly called me here, so I don't know exactly how long this is all going to take."

That seemed to be enough of a promise for Sprinkles, and he happily wagged his tail harder and pressed his face against the window of the passenger door of my car, trying to get out.

I shook my head at him in amusement, and made my way around to let him out of the car. I had a feeling that no matter how much I tried to resist, I was going to end up getting my dog's nails painted today.

Once we were inside, however, I quickly forgot any worries about nail polish. As soon as I opened the front door, my jaw dropped. To my great shock, Sydney Joyner was inside. She looked like she'd had a few too many glasses of champagne today, just as Trevor had at the party the night before. Her cheeks were flushed bright red, and she was waving around a stack of papers. In a slurry, drunken voice, she was screaming something about Alice being guilty, and saying that she couldn't believe that anyone was still okay with the fact that Alice was freely walking the streets.

Everyone in the salon was staring at her, most of them with their mouths gaping open. I myself could hardly believe what I was seeing. Even though I had already encountered Sydney once today and had seen that she wasn't as quiet as I'd always thought she was, I still couldn't believe that she was here, drunkenly telling the whole salon that Alice was guilty.

Unfortunately, because everyone was quiet and still except for Sydney, the noise I made when entering the room drew quite a bit of attention. When a few faces turned to look at me, Sydney turned around to see who had just joined her audience. Her eyes widened when she saw me, and then she threw back her head and let out a maniacal laugh.

"Did you go ask Alice about the chipped tooth? I hope you did, although I'm sure she tried to play it all down somehow. But she won't be able to escape the truth when I show Mitch these papers."

Sydney waved the papers around again, and let loose another maniacal laugh. I was growing tired of this game, and I looked over at Molly with questions in my eyes. Molly shrugged at me.

"I don't know exactly what she's talking about," Molly explained. "She just came in here a few minutes ago and started ranting that Alice was guilty and she could prove it to us. That's why I told you to get down here. But so far, she hasn't exactly offered any proof. She's just been ranting about the fact that Trevor was supposedly going to sue Alice for a chipped tooth."

"That is true," I admitted reluctantly. "Trevor threatened to sue Alice, although I'm not sure he had any basis for an actual lawsuit. It doesn't sound like Alice had done anything negligent. And anyway, I'm sure she had liability insurance that would have covered any accidents that happened in her café, so it's a bit of a stretch to say that Alice killed Trevor to avoid a lawsuit."

At this, Sydney started laughing like a crazy person again. "Oh, funny you should mention liability insurance. It just so happens that Alice had allowed her liability insurance to lapse. I have proof of that right here." She again waved the papers she was holding. "So, you see, Alice did have something to worry about if Trevor sued her."

For several moments, I stared at Sydney in shock, as did everyone else in the room. Then, a sudden surge of adrenaline rushed through me, and I reacted. I jumped toward Sydney to make a grab for the papers.

"Let me see those!" I yelped. But even though she'd clearly had too much to drink, Sydney had surprisingly quick reflexes. She jumped out of my way just in time, and clasped the papers tightly to her chest.

"Oh, no you don't," she roared. "These are mine. I'm going to take them and show them to Mitch. There's no way I'm handing them over to you. You'll just try to destroy them and continue this little game of acting like Alice is actually innocent."

What she was saying was ridiculous. If Alice truly had let her liability insurance lapse, it didn't matter whether I had the papers or Sydney had the papers or the Pope himself had the papers! The insurance company would have records of everything, and they would be able to verify that Alice had not had liability insurance.

My heart sank as I looked over at Sydney. I didn't know what to say. I only wanted to look at the papers so I could verify the truth of what Sydney was claiming. A small part of me held out hope that Sydney was just bluffing in an attempt to make everyone in here think that Alice was the one behind Trevor's drowning. But then, Sydney got a glint in her eyes, as though she understood what I was thinking.

"You can look at the papers," she said in a superior tone of voice. "But don't make another grab for them. If you try to touch me, I'll charge you with assault."

I wanted to tell her that she wouldn't have any luck getting an assault charge to stick to me, but I decided that it was best to play along with her little game for the moment. That way, I could actually see what she held in her hands.

I took a step closer, slowly, and Sydney held the papers up so I could read them. She kept a wary eye on me the whole time, and I was careful not to make any sudden moves. Instead, I slowly let my eyes scan over the words on the page. My heart sank further as I read. If these papers were indeed legitimate—and I had no reason to think that they weren't—then Sydney was right: Alice had let her liability insurance lapse three months ago, which meant that during the time Trevor had chipped his tooth, she had been uninsured. If he'd sued her and won, Alice wouldn't have had any insurance money to cover any settlement he might have received.

I silently cursed under my breath, wondering why in the world Alice hadn't told me this when I talked to her about ten minutes ago. So much for her not hiding anything else from me. She clearly didn't want to explain anything that might make her look bad. But how was I supposed to help her if I kept getting blindsided by evidence that spoke against her?

Sydney must have been able to see the despair on my face, and she let out a long, victorious laugh. "See? Alice is guilty. She had so many reasons to get rid of Trevor, and she was missing during the time he drowned. Mitch is going to have to arrest her, and any jury with two brain cells to rub together is going to convict her."

I didn't say anything. What could I say? In my heart, I still believed Alice was innocent. But I had to admit that Sydney had a point. The evidence didn't look so good for Alice.

I frowned and looked up at Sydney. "Where did you get these papers, anyway?"

She smirked at me. "Wouldn't you like to know? You're not the only one around here who knows how to play detective. I have ways of finding things out, too, and clearly my detective skills are superior to yours in this case. While you were running around trying to dig up dirt on Norman that doesn't exist, I found actual evidence against Alice. Mitch should hire me, and he should ban you from ever setting foot in the police station."

Sydney flipped her unruly hair over her shoulder again, then shook the papers in the air for everyone in the room to see. "I'm telling all of you: your beloved Alice isn't as innocent as you thought. I'm taking these to Mitch right now, and then you can forget about ever seeing her walking free again."

With that, Sydney turned around and sauntered out of the salon. Once again, silence hung over the room for several moments. Finally, one of the older women in the salon looked at me and timidly asked, "Is it true what she said? Did the papers really show that Alice had no liability insurance?"

"That's what those papers said," I admitted. "But I don't know if those papers are real or if they're some sort of fakes Sydney made up. Either way, I don't believe that Alice committed this crime. I still think she's innocent, even though there are things that look bad for her. She's just not the type to drown someone."

"But how can you say that with all of the evidence against her looking so bad?"

I paused before answering. It was a good question, and perhaps to some the answer might have sounded a bit ridiculous. But the truth was that it didn't matter to me what the evidence looked like. I knew in my heart that Alice was innocent. Perhaps that made me a horrible detective. Perhaps others would view me as burying my head in the sand and not following up on all leads properly like a good sleuth should.

But there was a difference between me and any outside observer to this case: I knew Alice. I'd gotten close to her over the last few months as we worked together to build our businesses. It seemed that she was going through a hard time financially, and I knew that money problems could make people go a little bit crazy. But no matter how crazy Alice went, I knew she could never go crazy enough to actually kill someone. At her core, she was just too good of a person.

I knew that wasn't the sort of "evidence" that would go over well in court. I might not have been a criminal lawyer, but I knew enough about criminal law to know that telling the jury that someone was a good person and couldn't possibly have killed someone wasn't going to get them off on a murder charge.

But knowing that Alice was a good person was enough for *me* to know that at the end of this investigation she would be found innocent. And so, I held my head high as I answered the woman who had just asked me the question.

"I know the evidence is piling up against her. But I also know Alice. I know that she would never hurt anyone, so no matter how much evidence there is that she did this, I'm still going to hold out hope that there's a reasonable explanation for all of it. I still believe she's innocent."

Once again, an uneasy silence hung over the room. I could tell that many in the salon were conflicted. Alice was well known in the community, and surely I wasn't the only one having trouble with the idea that she could have drowned someone. And yet, the doubtful looks on many faces told me that it was getting harder for everyone to ignore the evidence against her.

But what more could I say than what I already had? All I could do now was try my best to solve this case as quickly as possible. I had to prove to everyone that I was right, and that Alice was innocent.

But I felt a small flicker of doubt rising within me. I was right, wasn't I? I had been so sure of myself when I walked in here, but the way everyone was looking at me now made me wonder if I was being a fool. I was reminded of something my mother used to say to me: faces we see, but hearts we don't know.

Was it possible that behind the friendly, kind face Alice had been putting up that she had a black heart?

A small feeling of despair started rising within me, and no matter how hard I tried to shake it, I could tell that some doubts were taking root. I looked at Molly, desperately hoping that she would be looking back at me with an expression of reassurance, letting me know that she believed I was on the right track and that Alice was truly innocent.

But I saw doubt in Molly's eyes, too. How much evidence could pile up before I would be forced to completely lose my faith in Alice?

I gritted my teeth together. I wasn't sure of the answer to that question, but I did know that the evidence that had piled up thus far was not enough. Alice was innocent. I still believed that deep down in my heart.

At that moment, I heard Grams clear her throat from across the room. I looked up at where she sat in one of the salon chairs, getting her hair dyed a brilliant shade of hot pink. She smiled reassuringly at me in the way that only a grandmother could, and I instantly felt better.

"I, for one, am sure that Alice is innocent," Grams declared. She looked around the room with a defiant expression on her face, as though daring anyone to disagree with her. "We've all known Alice for a long time. She's practically a pillar of our community, and I'm not going to let this tragedy of Trevor's death change my opinion of her. It's horrible what happened to Trevor, but I know deep down that Alice isn't capable of that sort of violence. I think you all know it, too. So let's all calm down and let Izzy put her detective skills to work tracking down the real killer."

My heart leapt with gratitude, and I smiled at Grams as she smiled confidently back at me. But even though she had given my spirits a boost, I still felt weary. So far, this case seemed to only get worse for Alice the further I went into it. And Grams wasn't perfect. She *had* been wrong about people before. She'd defended people whom she'd said could never possibly be a murderer, but then they had indeed turned out to be murderers. How did I know that this time wasn't any different? Although I smiled bravely, I felt like a nervous wreck on the inside.

Molly must have seen these conflicting emotions on my face and known that it was time for me to get away from the prying eyes of everyone in the room. She stood and gave me a warm, confident smile.

"Well," she said. "One thing I do know for sure is that you've been working very hard on this case and you deserve a chance to relax. I'm just about done with my appointment here. Why don't you and I head down to the Sunshine Springs Winery's tasting room? They've got extended hours on Mondays now, and it's a beautiful evening. There's no sense in sitting around here moping. Let's go relax over a glass of Theo's best pinot."

I looked over at her gratefully. "That sounds amazing. Let's do that."

Then, beside me, I heard a small whine. I looked down to see Sprinkles looking dolefully up at me. I knew from the expression on his face that he wasn't happy about the fact that we were leaving before he'd had a chance to have his nails painted. Grams must have understood that that's what was bothering him as well, because she laughed and patted at the empty salon chair next to her.

"Come here, Sprinkles. Come to Grams. I'll make sure you get those nails taken care of while your mommy goes to drink wine."

Sprinkles looked up at me hopefully, and I nodded at him with a laugh. "Go on, then. Go enjoy some spa time while I head to the winery with Auntie Molly."

Sprinkles barked excitedly and took off to see Grams.

But I wasn't feeling quite so excited. Sure, I was happy to have the chance to spend time with Molly. But I felt that even the chance to rehash this case with my best friend wasn't going to make things better.

The only thing that was going to make this better was to find more conclusive evidence that Alice was innocent. And despite my attempts to display confidence to everyone at Sophia's Snips, I couldn't shake the worry that I might not be finding that evidence anytime soon. I hoped talking things through with Molly would help me see something in this case that I hadn't seen yet, because I was starting to feel a little desperate.

CHAPTER TWELVE

Apparently, Molly had been wrong about the fact that the winery had extended hours on Mondays, because when we arrived at the tasting room, the door was locked and the place was completely dark. There were a few cars in the parking lot, but I assumed those must have been from employees who were finishing up various tasks at the winery.

"Well, shoot," Molly said. "I could have sworn that I'd heard Theo was extending hours on Mondays now. But I guess I misunderstood."

My shoulders slumped slightly, but I put a bright smile on my face, anyway. "Don't worry. I've got plenty of wine at my house. Let's just head back there and do our own little tasting. We can still swing by my café and see if there's any strawberry moonshine pie left for you."

"Did someone say pie?"

I grinned before I even turned around. I would know that voice anywhere. Sure enough, when I looked over my shoulder, I saw Theo Russo standing there.

"Fancy meeting you here," I quipped.

Theo chuckled. "It is a bit crazy that I actually spend time on the grounds of the winery I own, isn't it?" he joked. "But what are you ladies doing here? Hopefully not planning to march up to my villa and accuse me of murdering Trevor?"

He laughed, but I groaned and Molly winced. When I'd first moved to Sunshine Springs, Molly and I had been convinced that Theo had been the one to murder a girl who had died outside of my café. We'd been so convinced of it, in fact, that we'd come to his villa at about ten o'clock one night to bang on the door and demand that he turn himself in to the police. The whole thing seemed so ridiculous looking back on it that, even now, months later, I felt my cheeks heating up with embarrassment at the memory.

Somehow, despite this rocky start, Theo and I had become good friends. He even wanted to date me, although I'd told him a thousand times that I wasn't interested in a relationship.

"You're never going to let us live that one down, are you?" Molly asked.

Theo beamed. "Nope. It's too good of a story to let it die. But since you're both here, would you like to come back to the villa with me and have some wine? It just so happens that I actually have one of Izzy's strawberry moonshine pies at my house as well."

I looked up at him in surprise. "You have a whole pie? That seems like a random purchase."

Theo laughed again, and the musical sound of that laughter seemed to carry far into the night. "Well, I'm not the one who actually bought it. One of my would-be girlfriends bought it for me as a gift. She'd heard it was my favorite flavor and thought that she might butter me up by bringing me one."

Molly raised an eyebrow at him. "Is the strawberry moonshine really your favorite flavor?"

Theo shrugged. "Personally, I think death by chocolate is better. But I won't say no to any of Izzy's pies, especially when I get them for free." He winked at me.

I rolled my eyes at him. "I pretty much give you whatever pie you want for free anytime you come in. But to answer your question, yes, as long as Molly is interested as well, I'd love to sit and have some pie with you at your villa."

I looked expectantly over at Molly, and she shrugged and nodded. "Why not? I was planning on being out here for a while. I thought the winery had extended hours tonight?" She looked at Theo, and he shook his head.

"We actually just ended our extended hours Monday experiment tonight. We've done it for a few weeks now to try to make an event out of it and extend the weekend business a bit. But it turns out that people actually aren't that interested in staying out late and drinking on Monday. They're still too worn out from the weekend, I suppose. We've had a few patrons here and there, but not enough to make keeping the tasting room open worth it."

"Well, I'm glad we ran into you then, so that this trip wasn't wasted," Molly said.

"It's never a waste to come out to the Sunshine Springs Winery!" Theo declared. "Now, come on. We can sit by the fountain outside my villa. The weather is crazy warm for a November night, and it would be a shame to waste such a beautiful evening." He winked at me. "I even promise not to drown either of you."

Molly groaned, and I punched him in the arm. "That's not funny!" I said. "Don't be so irreverent!"

He didn't look the least bit contrite. Instead, he gave me a playful punch back and grinned. "Mitch tells me that you're determined to work on this case whether he wants you to or not. He didn't seem too happy about that fact."

I made a face. "Mitch is such a fair-weather friend. On the last murder case, when he needed my help, he was all 'Please Izzy, can you help me? Oh thank you Izzy. I don't know what I'd do without you!' And now, when he doesn't think he needs my help, he acts like I'm causing him such a headache by insisting on chasing down clues."

Theo raised his hands in a gesture of surrender. "Hey, don't shoot the messenger. I'm just telling you what Mitch told me. I'm actually quite interested to see what you've been turning up on this case."

Molly laughed. "That's why you're offering pie and wine. You think you can bribe us into talking about what we know."

Theo looked over at her and grinned. "Can you blame me for trying? Besides, I've found that bribing with pie and wine tends to be highly effective. It just might work."

"It just might," I said. "To be honest, I would love to hear what both of you have to say about how this case is going. The evidence keeps pointing toward Alice, but I just can't believe that she's guilty. And there are a few things to make Norman look suspicious."

Theo looked intrigued. "I can't wait to hear about this. But hold that thought. First, let me get the pie and wine. Then you can tell us everything you know, and we'll do our best to help you sort it all out."

Several minutes later, we were sitting at a small table near a large fountain that decorated part of the expansive yard outside of Theo's villa. The villa was located just down a long gravel road past the winery's tasting room, and I'd sat out here by the fountain dozens of times since moving to Sunshine Springs. But no matter how many times I was there, I could never forget what it had been like the first day I sat by the fountain.

Theo had brought me here after giving me a tour of his winery. He'd made it clear at that point that he wanted to date me, and for a brief moment in time I had considered actually saying yes to this suggestion. I'd certainly been considering it when we sat out there that first day by the fountain. It had been a hot, sunny day, but we'd been under the shade of an orange tree, and it had seemed like a bit of a modern fairytale moment. Theo had leaned in to kiss me, but just as he had, we were interrupted by Mitch rushing forward to let Theo know that he was a suspect in a murder case.

Theo's lips had never actually met mine, and I'd never been able to summon up the bravery to let him try again. Instead, I'd kept him at arms' length, just like I'd kept Mitch at arms' length. Now, I tried not to think about those memories as I accepted a slice of strawberry moonshine pie from Theo. He'd already poured glasses of wine for everyone, and he held his up for a toast.

"Cheers, to nights with friends where no one ends up dead."

"The night is young," I pointed out. "Don't jinx us."

Molly didn't find any of this funny, and I guess I couldn't blame her for that. Joking about death right after a murder wasn't the best idea, but that's the way Theo was. He often dealt with stressful situations through humor.

"Enough with the jokes," Molly said after she'd taken a bite of pie. "I want to hear what Izzy has learned on this case so far."

As quickly as I could, I brought them up to speed on everything I'd discovered. They were as surprised as I was to hear that Norman had been sneaking around Cody's office, and they both agreed that this looked suspicious. But neither of them had any ideas as to what Norman might have been looking for.

"Let me guess," Theo said. "You haven't mentioned anything to Mitch about seeing Norman in Cody's office?"

"Not yet," I said, a bit defensively. "But I will. I was just trying to sort through my thoughts on everything before talking to him."

Theo laughed. "I think you mean you were trying to solve the case quickly before talking to Mitch about it so that you can get all the credit. Don't try to deny it."

He was right, and I didn't try to deny it. Instead, I shrugged. "Well, I will admit that was my original intent with waiting to talk to Mitch. But I'm starting to feel like this case is going to take forever to solve. And to make matters worse, Alice won't be straight with me about things. She dances around all the issues and I end up finding out incriminating evidence against her from other people. Like Sydney Joyner."

Theo frowned at this. "It seems a little strange to me that Sydney is so interested in how this turns out. Why does she care whether the murder was committed by Norman or by Alice?

"It's a good question," Molly piped in. "Scott told me that she was quite upset about Trevor's death when she drove home. I think it's because she works so closely with the candidates for mayor, since she's in charge of the election process here in Sunshine Springs. She gets to know them pretty well, and it's probably devastating to have someone that you know so well die. It would only make things worse to have another person she knows well be considered a murder suspect. She's probably a bit overwhelmed at the moment."

"I get that," I said. "But I still think it's strange how antagonistic she's been toward me."

"Do you think there's something more there?" Theo asked. "Maybe she knows something else about Alice that she's not letting on yet?"

I frowned. I hated to consider this possibility. I just wanted something that would prove Alice's innocence, but even as I had this thought, I knew I had to stop going about my investigation that way. If the clues led to Alice, then I needed to follow them. If I truly believed she was innocent, then I shouldn't be afraid to follow those clues. They would only prove Alice's innocence in the end, and perhaps they would lead me to clues that might show me who the true murderer was.

At least, that's what I hoped. So why couldn't I shake that uneasy feeling that I wasn't going to like what I found if I looked more into Alice? I had to admit that my faith in her was starting to crumble. Thankfully, Theo chose that moment to speak again and distract me from these troublesome thoughts.

"You know, I don't know what Norman was looking for in Cody's office, but I do have to say that Cody must be quite stressed out. He's been ordering a ridiculous amount of wine from the winery recently. He must be drinking at least two bottles a night."

I looked at Theo and frowned. "That doesn't seem probable. He doesn't act like an alcoholic. Maybe he's having a lot of parties? Or maybe he's just trying to build up his wine collection?"

Theo shrugged. "I don't know what he's doing with all that wine. I just know that he's buying quite a bit of it. I originally thought that it was for events that Trevor was holding as part of his publicity campaign, but Cody still ordered the wine this week even though Trevor is obviously no longer in the running for mayor."

"Hmm," I said. "I wonder if Norman and Cody were part of a conspiracy against Trevor. Or maybe Cody knew that Norman was planning to hurt Trevor. Do you think Cody had some documents to prove this and Norman is worried that Cody will show them to Mitch?"

"Wait. What about Cody himself?" Molly asked with a frown. "Are we missing the obvious suspect here? If he was so involved with everything, is it possible that he himself is the one who killed Trevor?"

I shook my head. "I don't think so. Mitch questioned everyone who had been speaking with Trevor that night. If Cody had been missing and didn't have an alibi during the time that the drowning took place, Mitch would have added him to the suspect list. Mitch questioned a lot of people outside the library, but he only took Norman and Alice down to the station for statements. I don't think anyone else at the party was a suspect. Of course, I can't rule out that someone who was *not* at the party was part of things. But so far the only evidence anyone has found has pointed to Norman or Alice."

Theo and Molly both shrugged, and didn't seem to have much of a response to that.

I gulped back the last of my wine and stood. "I should get going. I hate to break up this party early but I have a lot to do at the café tomorrow."

Molly stood with me. "I guess I'm also going, since Izzy is my ride."

"I'm happy to drive you back to town or have one of my vineyard guys do it for you if you want to hang out and eat more pie," Theo told her.

But Molly shook her head. "No, thank you. I have a lot of stuff I should get done, too. But I appreciate the offer."

Theo nodded, then stood and gave us both goodbye hugs. As we walked back in the direction of the tasting room's parking lot, Molly and I were both silent. I didn't know what thoughts might be going through Molly's head, but I knew that I myself was feeling quite dejected.

After a few minutes of silence, I was about to finally say something to Molly when the sound of low voices caught my ear. I glanced over at Molly, wondering if she'd heard it too, and she raised an eyebrow at me to indicate she had.

Something about the way the voices were speaking sounded suspicious. Theo had already said that he'd closed the tasting room earlier than he'd originally intended tonight, so any tourists or other customers who were here for tastings should have been long gone. The only people still hanging around were Theo's employees, and why would any of them be sneaking around and speaking in whispers?

Molly must have also felt that the voices seemed suspicious, because she motioned me over to hide behind a large stack of wine barrels. I nodded and followed her, and we crouched down to try to listen. The voices seemed to be getting closer, but I still couldn't make out what they were saying. At least as they approached our hiding spot I could tell that the voices belonged to a man and a woman. I could also tell that the man and woman were giggling in that sort of way that lovers often do.

I let out a small sigh and relaxed. This was probably just a couple sneaking around thinking it was romantic to walk through the winery at night. Nothing sinister was going on here.

But just as I was about to stand up and keep walking—after all, I wasn't going to hide because of a giggling, tipsy couple—Molly pulled me back down.

"Are you out of your mind?" she asked. "Don't let them see you."

I looked at her in confusion, not understanding why she would think I shouldn't let these people see me. But then, I looked again in the direction her finger was pointing, and I had to hold back a gasp.

This wasn't just any couple sneaking through the vineyard. This was Norman and Sydney, their fingers intertwined and their bodies far too close for anyone to think that there wasn't something romantic going on between them.

Suddenly, Sydney's motivation for making sure that Norman wasn't convicted of murder made so much more sense. Of course she didn't want him to go to jail for murder if she was in love with him.

I glanced at Molly again, and she looked back at me with wide eyes. We both sat perfectly still, and strained our ears to hear what the two of them were saying. As they got closer, I could finally could make out their actual words.

Unfortunately, what they were saying didn't seem to have much to do with Trevor's murder case. Instead, they were whispering embarrassingly cheesy sweet nothings to each other. I felt awkward sitting there listening in, but Molly and I didn't have a choice now. There was no way we could leave our hiding spot without Norman and Sydney realizing that we'd been hiding, so we were stuck, hoping they wouldn't notice us and would quickly pass on by.

But the pace they were moving at was anything but quick. They paused right in front of us, and my heart pounded in my chest. I was sure they were going to look over and realize that two women were hiding behind the wine barrels. But they were too wrapped up in each other to notice us. Instead, they embraced, and Norman planted a big kiss on Sydney's lips.

I felt my cheeks heat up with embarrassment. I was mortified that I was accidentally witnessing this. When I glanced over at Molly, her face was bright red, and I knew she felt the same way. Still, we were stuck until they walked far enough away that we could leave our hiding spot without being seen.

One thing I knew for sure: Norman had already been on the top of my suspect list, but now I was convinced he was the murderer. Clearly, Sydney had just been trying to distract from the fact that there was evidence against Norman by bringing up everything she could against Alice. Why hadn't I realized that before? It had never occurred to me that the head of the elections committee would date one of the candidates for mayor. That was obviously a huge conflict of interest.

It was also a huge indication that Norman had not been conducting himself in a manner that respected the law. I felt a rush of relief as I realized that this boded well for Alice. Surely, any motivation she might have had to harm Trevor would be dwarfed by the revelation that the current mayor was involved with the head of the elections committee.

My excitement grew as I realized the possibilities. Had Trevor discovered this conflict of interest and threatened to expose them? That would have been a huge motivation for Norman to get rid of Trevor. Norman wouldn't have been looking just at the loss of his position as mayor, but also at charges of election fraud. I could imagine that he would have been desperate to keep his indiscretions from being revealed.

I was already making plans to go investigate this further as Norman and Sydney started walking away. But as they walked, hand-in-hand, their conversation turned a bit more serious than it had been. I turned my ear toward them and strained to hear as best I could.

"Do you think she is going to lay off of things now?" Norman asked. In the moonlight, I could make out a slight shrug of Sydney's shoulders.

"I hope so. I showed her the papers proving that Alice let her liability insurance lapse. And I did double check that those papers are real, so if she does try to follow up on them, she'll find out that they're legitimate."

"Well, I hope you're right and that Izzy looks more closely at Alice and not at us. We can't afford to be looked at too closely."

Norman sounded angry, and I felt a wave of shock go through me at his words. What was he talking about? Had he just admitted that there was evidence against him? I strained even harder to hear, desperate to know what the details were.

"Ain't that the truth," Sydney said. "The last thing we need right now is Mitch poking around in our business. Did you get all of the papers and folders from Cody's office?"

"Yes, and I'll destroy them all first thing in the morning. I just want to go through them first to make sure that I have everything before I destroy it all. We can't be too careful."

At that point, they walked out of earshot again, and their voices became mere murmurs once more. But I had heard enough. I looked at Molly and saw that her jaw had dropped.

"Did you hear all that?" I hissed in a whisper, even though it was clear from the expression on her face that she had.

She looked pale. "Yes, I heard it. But Izzy, they're heading straight for the parking lot."

I frowned, not seeing what this had to do with anything. "So? That's where they're parked, I'm sure. I didn't notice Sydney's car when I came in because I don't actually know what she drives. They must not have taken Norman's vehicle. I would have recognized his bright yellow truck right away."

And then, it suddenly hit me what Molly was saying. I slapped my hand over my mouth in horror. "Oh, no! My car is in the parking lot."

"Exactly," Molly said. "If they see it they're going to know you're around here somewhere. They might figure out that we're onto them."

"What should we do?" I asked.

Molly shrugged in resignation. "What can we do? Either they notice the car or they don't. It's too late to go move it now."

"I have to at least see whether they recognize it. I have to know whether they know that I'm onto them."

Before Molly could say anything else, I started creeping along the wall. I heard a slight sigh behind me, and I knew Molly thought I was crazy. Perhaps I was. Perhaps taking a chance on exposing myself was not the smartest thing I could do right now. But I had to know if Norman and Sydney were going to realize I was there. If they did, it was going to be a race against time to let Mitch know he needed to get down to Norman's office and get those papers. I was one hundred percent confident that if Norman realized that I knew everything he'd just said, that he would go destroy the papers immediately.

I tried to be as quiet as I could, but I had to move quickly. I could see that Sydney and Norman were not moseying quite as slowly as they had been before. I managed to get close enough to the parking lot so that I had a good vantage point, but was still mostly hidden behind some grapevines. If Norman or Sydney had looked directly at Molly and me, they probably would have noticed our shadows. But we weren't that noticeable unless you were actually looking for us, and, at the moment, Norman and Sydney were not looking for anyone. They had gone back to their giggling, romantic mush-fest, and seemed to only be interested in gazing into each other's eyes.

This was good news for me. It meant that they weren't paying attention to which cars were in the parking lot. I kept my fingers crossed the entire time they were walking back to their car, giggling and pausing now and then for a quick kiss. They got into their car, still laughing, and I made a mental note that Sydney drove a bright red sedan. Once in the car, she sped out of the parking lot quickly, eager to get to their next destination.

I uncrossed my fingers and let out the breath I'd been holding. "I don't think they noticed my car."

Molly shook her head. "I don't think so. In fact, I don't think they would have noticed a man in a gorilla suit if he'd walked right in front of them. They're clearly quite taken with each other."

I stood up and started walking toward my car, with Molly following me.

"I have to find out what's in those papers," I said. "I don't know how Cody and Norman both have managed to hide them from the searches that I'm sure Mitch has done at their offices, but I'm convinced that whatever is in those papers will prove that Norman had a strong motive to kill Trevor."

Molly frowned at me as we both climbed into my car and buckled our seatbelts. "But how will you get into Norman's office? I'm sure security is pretty tight at the government building where the mayor's office is located, and I don't think that Norman's going to invite you in for tea anytime soon."

I had already been considering this. "I think I know someone who can give me access."

I floored the accelerator on my car as I headed back toward town. I felt excitement mounting within me as I considered the possibility that I might actually solve this case tonight. Meanwhile, Molly was still looking at me with a confused expression on her face.

I smiled confidently back at her. "Can you dig my cell phone out of my purse for me? I have a phone call to make."

CHAPTER THIRTEEN

Forty-five minutes later, I was standing inside the reception area of the mayor's office, trying not to look too triumphant. As I'd hoped, Norman's receptionist had eaten up every line I'd fed her about needing to investigate Norman's office for his own safety. I told her that I was working on the case—I just didn't mention that I wasn't working on it in an *official* capacity.

Norman's secretary had already shown that she considered me someone who cared about Norman, so she hadn't questioned me too much. She'd only been confused as to why I couldn't wait until the morning to speak with Norman directly. I made up some story that I was worried that the murderer might strike again if he wasn't stopped right away.

I felt a little bit guilty, but not overly so. I made myself feel better by telling myself that whatever I found here, I would immediately take to Mitch. I had no doubt that he would still be at the police station working, even though it was getting late. When he had a murder case this fresh, he tended to be at the office quite late. I was already smiling as I imagined walking into his office and proudly depositing concrete evidence on his desk that Norman had been involved in all sorts of unsavory things.

First though, I had to figure out exactly what those things were that he shouldn't have been involved in.

Norman's receptionist looked uneasily around after she let me in, and then glanced at her watch.

"I'll be quick, I promise," I said, worried that she was going to change her mind before I even had a chance to get started.

She fidgeted slightly. "Oh, I don't want to rush you. I know what you're doing is important. It's just that I had a date to go see a nine P.M. movie with this guy I really like and if I don't get going soon…"

I glanced at my watch. It was eight-forty-five. If she didn't leave now, she was going to be late for the movie. I felt badly, but I didn't want to come back again the next day. That would be too late!

"I'll be quick, I promise. I can take what I need with me to look at and then bring it back in the morning."

I was already making plans to dump as many folders as I could in a pile and take them with me. Norman would be furious when he arrived in the morning to discover so many missing folders, but he wouldn't have much of a leg to stand on with his fury if I had evidence that he had been involved in fraud and murder.

But Norman's secretary was shaking her head. "I really don't want to rush you. Do you think maybe I could just leave my key with you and you could lock up when you leave? I could swing by the Drunken Pie Café in the morning on my way to work and get the key from you. I know you get in really early, so you should already be there by the time I'm on my way to work, right?"

For a few beats, I just stared at her. I felt an immense wave of guilt wash over me when I realized how incredibly trusting she was being with me. I was totally screwing her boss over, and she thought I was trying to help him.

But I pushed the guilt down. It wasn't my fault that her boss had gotten himself involved in a murder case. I was pretty sure he was the killer, so why should I feel guilty about this? Surely, once this girl realized what was going on, she'd be glad she'd helped me.

I quickly recovered my wits and nodded. "That would be fine. I'm always at the café well before the rest of the town wakes up, so I'm sure I'll be there when you swing by."

Her face lit up, and she surprised me by giving me a quick hug. "Oh, thank you so much, Izzy! I feel ridiculous even asking, but you know how it is when you like a guy…"

I grinned at her. "I know. Now shoo! Get out of here and have fun."

And stop making me feel guilty that I'm not being entirely truthful with you.

When the receptionist was gone, I quickly began looking through the office. Even though she'd told me to take as much time as I needed, I wasn't going to dillydally. I didn't know how long my luck would hold out. If the wrong person came through here and questioned me—say an overzealous security guard—this operation might be shut down immediately. Anyone who thought to call Mitch and ask why I was the one investigating instead of an official police officer would quickly find out that I had no actual authority to be here. I hadn't even brought Molly with me, because explaining why she was tagging along would have been too difficult. Molly had made me promise to update her as soon as I could, but she had understood.

I was disappointed to see that the folders Norman had taken from Cody's office were no longer sitting out in the open on the bookshelf where they'd been earlier. I wasn't surprised, though. Whatever information those green folders contained wasn't something Norman wanted anyone to find. I began quickly sifting through piles of paper and folders in his office, looking for what he'd taken. But after several long minutes of searching, I wasn't having much luck.

Norman had several cabinets that locked, and I realized that the folders I was looking for were probably in there. I groaned, thinking that I should have thought of that, and wondered how hard these locks would be to pick.

I was by no means a talented lock-picker. The most I'd ever done was pick the lock of the bathroom door when a toddler I'd been babysitting for a friend had angrily locked himself in there. I didn't think that experience qualified me to consider myself an expert, but it looked like I was going to have to at least make an attempt.

Then, I looked down at the keychain Norman's secretary had given me and saw that there were several keys hanging on it in addition to the one she'd used to open the office. Was it possible one of them opened the cabinets?

Hardly daring to hope that I'd be so lucky, I started trying the keys. The first two did not fit at all, but the third one opened the cabinet.

"Yes!" I exclaimed as I pulled the cabinet's door open. Unfortunately, the folders I was looking for weren't in there. I moved on to the next locked cabinet. This one took a different key, but that key was also on the keychain. I went through three locked cabinets, and was beginning to think that perhaps Norman had somehow already known to move the folders out of his office.

But there was one more cabinet left for me to try, and I quickly found a key on the keychain that opened it. As I started sifting through the papers, I felt my heart dropping. This looked like a bunch of boring utility contracts. There was nothing in here to implicate Norman in any kind of crime.

I started to panic a bit. Had I misunderstood something? Had Norman not been involved in some sort of scandal or illegal activity? Was I wasting my time here, and worse, was I going to come away empty-handed? In the morning, Norman's secretary was sure to tell him I'd been here. If I hadn't already found something to bring to Mitch, Norman was going to explode with anger—and I would have no reasonable way to defend myself.

I flipped through the papers in the cabinet faster and faster, and was about to give up in despair when I realized that there were some folders shoved in the very back of the cabinet that looked quite similar to the green folders I'd seen Norman taking from Cody's office. I tried to stay calm, knowing that it might just be a coincidence that the folders were the same color. But I couldn't fully contain my excitement at the possibility that I might have just found something.

When I opened up the folders and started flipping through the papers inside, I could see that they definitely weren't utility contracts. As my eyes scanned the printouts, I saw quite a bit of information on how the ballot system in Sunshine Springs worked. There were detailed instructions for logging into the electronic counting system to make changes. But not only that, there were several handwritten notes alongside the printed information. The notes were in a flowery script that looked like it must have come from a woman, and gave detailed, added information to supplement the printouts. Unsurprisingly, these notes weren't signed, but I had a pretty good feeling they came from Sydney. Many of the notes said things like *"we can change this to help you"* or *"this would give you a boost in the final tally."*

But a note on the final page was what truly made me believe the notes were from Sydney to Norman. I saw a handwritten message that read *"Don't worry! We're going to beat him."* The note was signed *"Xoxo"* with a little drawing of a heart next to it.

I supposed that Mitch would have to have someone look at these and do an official handwriting analysis on it to know whether it actually came from Sydney, but I would have been willing to place a pretty hefty bet on the fact that she was behind these notes. I felt my heart pounding faster as I flipped through the pages in the folders again. These would no doubt prove that Sydney and Norman had been in some sort of conspiracy to rig the election. If Cody had discovered these, then he had probably been trying to use the papers as blackmail. Perhaps he'd been trying to get Norman to drop out of the race completely?

And it was likely that Cody had shared all of this information with Trevor as well. Had Norman killed Trevor to avoid having his plans to falsify election results revealed?

I frowned. This seemed like a likely possibility. Certainly much likelier than the possibility that Alice had killed Trevor in an attempt to keep him from suing her over a chipped tooth, and definitely more likely than the possibility that Alice had killed Trevor to keep him from shutting down her café for making homemade chocolate. At least, it seemed that way to me.

Still, I wasn't sure why, if Norman had killed Trevor to keep this secret quiet, that he hadn't killed Cody as well. If Cody had this information, then he could have made Norman's life miserable even though Trevor was dead. But perhaps Norman had figured that if he took the papers from Cody, then Cody wouldn't be able to make anyone believe that Norman had been intending to cause election fraud. Norman had been mayor for a while, and he hadn't been involved in any scandals thus far. It probably would have seemed like quite a stretch for him to suddenly commit such a huge scandal and then commit murder to keep that scandal quiet.

To be honest, I too might have thought it was crazy a few days ago. But that was before I had seen Norman kissing Sydney, and heard him talking about how these very papers in front of me needed to be destroyed. Clearly, he wasn't as innocent as he seemed.

There were still a few pieces of this puzzle to be sorted out, but those details would be figured out eventually. The important thing right now was that I had discovered proof that Norman had been participating in election fraud, which gave him a strong motive for killing Trevor. This was good news for Alice, and meant that I might actually be proving her innocence before she got charged, after all.

For a moment, I debated what to do with the papers. Should I grab them all and go, or should I make photocopies and leave the originals here so that if Mitch didn't get here before Norman, Norman still wouldn't suspect anything? But then, if Norman did destroy the originals before Mitch got to them, would that be a big blow to the case?

I knew everything would seem more legitimate if Mitch came in here and found the papers himself, but I wasn't sure I wanted to take the chance that the papers would be gone by the time he got to them. As I was struggling with the decision, I suddenly heard a sound in the hallway. My senses were instantly on alert, and my heart once again started pounding wildly in my chest. I wondered for a moment if Norman's secretary was returning, but that seemed unlikely. She'd seemed pretty excited about her date, and if she was coming back now she had definitely not gone on that date. But who else would be out in the hallway at this time of night? The government employees in Sunshine Springs weren't exactly known for staying in the office past five P.M.

I didn't have a lot of time to think about it. All I knew in that moment was that I needed to get out of there before someone saw me. Norman might be coming back now to destroy the papers. If he had indeed been the one to kill Trevor, as I strongly suspected, then he probably wouldn't have any qualms about killing me as well.

Without pausing to think about it any longer, I grabbed the folders, shut the cabinet quickly, and darted out into the main reception area of the mayor's office. I closed and locked Norman's office door itself, realizing then that I hadn't actually locked the cabinet. I couldn't worry about that right now, though. Yes, it would look suspicious that the cabinet was unlocked, but it's not like Norman wasn't going to realize someone had been in there once he actually opened the cabinet and saw that all the folders were missing. The most important thing for me right now was just to get out of there.

With my heart pounding in my chest, I peeked out the window of the reception area. I didn't see anyone at the moment, but that didn't necessarily make me feel better. I'd definitely heard someone out here, and my first guess as to who it was would be Norman. My second guess would be Sydney. I didn't want to meet either of them here in a dark, empty office building.

Clutching the folders to my chest, I decided to make a run for it. Going out into the hallway with Norman or Sydney out there might be dangerous, but staying behind here trapped in the office wasn't any safer. I was like a sitting duck, just waiting for someone to come get me.

Taking a deep breath, I stepped into the hallway and looked around. I didn't see anyone, so I quickly locked the door to the office. If I left the door unlocked and anything got stolen, I didn't want the secretary to get in trouble, since she was the one who'd given me the key. Of course, as far as Norman was concerned, the most important thing in the office had already been stolen. But I wasn't exactly thinking rationally at that moment.

I was running on the biggest rush of adrenaline I'd ever felt, and I found it impossible to think clearly. The only thought that I could really latch onto was that I needed to get to Mitch. Hopefully, he'd still be at the station working late. If not, I was sure he'd be interested in meeting up with me despite the late hour. I had quite a bit to tell him about the case.

I just had to make it to him alive.

With the door locked and the coast apparently clear, I took off toward the building's exit, trying to balance being as quiet as possible with moving as quickly as possible. I wasn't sure that I had found the right balance, but I was doing my best to escape quickly without sounding like a herd of rhinoceroses. As I rounded the corner of the hallway, I breathed a little easier.

Had I just imagined the noise in the hallway? Perhaps it had been something benign like a janitor making a late night pass through the building to clean things up a bit. I took a deep breath and let it out slowly, telling myself to calm down and stop being so ridiculous. Clearly, I had been overreacting. There was no one anywhere near Norman's office right now except me.

I smiled, feeling amused now by my own ridiculousness. But just as I turned to continue heading toward the exit, my heart nearly stopped beating altogether.

There, coming down the hallway straight toward Norman's office, was a figure dressed all in black—including a black ski mask. I tried to see whether I could figure out who this person was by the way their eyes looked, but in the dim light I couldn't make out anything more than the outline of their body.

One thing I did know, however, was that this person wasn't up to anything good. People wearing black ski masks usually weren't.

In addition to the black ski mask, the intruder wore a huge pair of black sweatpants, and a huge black hoodie. I forced myself not to let out a scream as I saw the intruder trying the door handle on the front reception area of Norman's office. Of course it was locked, since I'd just locked it a few moments before. But I couldn't shake the realization that if I had stayed just a few minutes longer in the office, this person would have found me there. I shivered at how close of a call that had been. I told myself to run, but I stood frozen in that spot, peering at the intruder as they reached into their pocket and pulled out a set of keys.

That's when I turned and fled. If this person had keys to the office, then they must have been someone who belonged there. So why the ski mask and hooded getup? The only explanation I could come up with was that this was Norman and he wanted to get the papers I clutched to my chest right now without anyone knowing it was him. I was sure there were security cameras in the office. I hadn't worried that much about them because I figured the secretary had unlocked the door for me, so I technically wasn't breaking in. Besides, who could be angry at me for finding information that would prove that Norman had murdered Trevor?

But Norman wouldn't have wanted any evidence that he'd been here and had been removing things from the office, in case someone came looking for them. Was that Norman hiding behind a ski mask, attempting to keep his identity secret as he removed the folders?

I couldn't know for sure, and I wasn't waiting around to find out. It was time to get these papers to Mitch, and to let him know that he needed to send some officers down to the mayor's office to intercept Trevor's true murderer.

CHAPTER FOURTEEN

I took off at a run out of the building, not worrying anymore about how loud I was being. Time was the only thing that mattered now. I drove my car as quickly as I could to the Sunshine Springs Police Station, praying that Mitch would be there.

When I pulled into the parking lot, I was happy to see that there were several cars there, including Mitch's. I'd been trying to call him on my phone while driving over, but he hadn't been answering. I'd tried both his cell phone and the main line for the police station, but I hadn't received any response. Because of that, I had half expected the station to be empty when I got there, and I was relieved to see that that wasn't the case.

When I opened the front door to the police station, I realized why no one had answered the main line: there was no one at the reception desk, which shouldn't have been all that surprising since it was pretty late by now. However, there was a police officer sitting on one of the couches in the reception area. He had several papers spread over a glass coffee table, and he appeared to be puzzling over those papers while also drinking copious amounts of coffee. He looked up in surprise when he saw me.

"Izzy? What are you doing here this late? What's wrong? You look awfully pale."

"I need to see Mitch!" I exclaimed, then started running toward the hallway that led to Mitch's office without bothering to wait for permission. The stunned officer in the reception area didn't manage to formulate any sort of reply before I had completely disappeared down the hallway.

When I reached Mitch's office, the door was closed. I was tempted to barge right in, but I managed to restrain myself. I didn't want to be rude, and besides, Mitch probably had a gun on him. He was usually pretty calm and wasn't the type to shoot a round without knowing who or what he was shooting at, even if someone did unexpectedly run into his office. But I didn't want to take any chances that he might be in an especially jumpy mood tonight, so I knocked.

Well, *knock* might be a bit of a tame description for what I did. Pounded on the door as hard as I could was more like it.

"Mitch! Mitch, open up! It's Izzy!"

A few seconds later, the door swung wide open and Mitch looked at me like I was out of my mind. Perhaps I was, but I had good reason to be.

"Izzy? Are you alright? What's going on?" I saw Mitch's eyes quickly scan from the top of my head to the bottom of my feet, looking for any sort of injury.

I quickly reassured him. "I'm fine. But I have big news. I've been trying to call you for the last ten minutes but I couldn't get through to your cell phone, or to the station's main line."

Mitch frowned and glanced back toward his phone, which sat on his desk but was facedown. "Oh, sorry. I put my phone on silent for a while because I was trying to work through some things without getting distracted. It's hard to focus when you're constantly being pinged. And we don't have a receptionist here right now, so since I wasn't answering the phone, all the station's calls just went to voicemail."

"Yeah, I noticed. Anyway, that doesn't matter now. The important thing is that I've discovered that Norman is the killer."

This got Mitch's attention. His jaw dropped as he stared back at me in silence for a few stunned seconds before finally speaking. "What? Are you sure? I had just about ruled him out. Did you find some new evidence?"

I nodded vigorously and pushed the stack of folders I was holding into his arms. "Norman was actually involved in a secret relationship with Sydney, whom you may remember is head of the elections committee in Sunshine Springs."

Mitch nodded slowly. I was thankful that he seemed so interested in what I was telling him that he hadn't yet commented on the fact that I'd been sleuthing around when he'd asked me not to. It's not like he hadn't known that I would do this, though. I'd made it pretty clear that I wanted to help Alice, and I had to admit that I was feeling quite a bit of pride right now that I actually had helped her. My excitement only grew as I continued speaking.

"Molly and I overheard Norman and Sydney talking—and kissing—at the winery earlier tonight. Norman told Sydney that he had papers in his office he needed to destroy, and I had actually seen Norman stealing papers a few a days ago from Cody's office. Long story short, I convinced Norman's secretary to let me into the mayor's office to search for the papers and—"

"You *what?*" Mitch interrupted. "How in the world did you manage that?"

I wasn't sure if his tone was one of admiration or disgust, but I decided I would worry about that later. Right now, I wanted to get my story out, so I ignored his question. "I looked for the papers that I knew Norman had stolen and I found them. The papers prove that Norman and Sydney were planning a big election fraud, which I'm sure you'll agree makes it pretty clear that, if Trevor had found out about this, Norman had a motive to get rid of Trevor."

"Hold on a minute," Mitch said, cracking his knuckles and clearly trying to contain his frustration. "You have to slow down. This is a lot to take in. Tell me everything you know from the beginning. And tell me slowly, without leaving any details out."

I nodded, and told Mitch as completely as possible everything that I'd learned over the last few days. Mitch listened without any comments, although he did make a few notes on a notepad as I spoke. He also cracked his knuckles again several times. When I finished, Mitch stared at me for several long moments in silence, a big frown turning down the corners of his lips. Finally, he let out a long sigh and spoke. "Well, this does present pretty convincing evidence against Norman. But it's not a slam dunk. There are still quite a few things to confirm. I'll have to—"

A loud squawking from Mitch's radio interrupted us. Mitch looked over at it quickly, and jumped out of his chair to grab it from the desk where it sat.

"Sorry, hang on. I'll need to take this. I have the radio set up so my officers can only contact me if they page the emergency channel. There must be something important going on. I'm going to run out to the front and talk to the guy sitting in the reception area, since I'll probably need his help if there truly is an emergency. You sit tight for a moment. I want to finish talking to you when I get back."

Mitch disappeared down the hallway, and I heard him bellowing, "This is Mitch!" into the radio before he stepped into the reception area and I could no longer hear him.

I fidgeted in my seat for several minutes, wishing Mitch would hurry up and return. At some point, I began to wonder if he'd forgotten about me. I started to think that I should go out to the front of the office and check. He clearly hadn't wanted me involved in whatever emergency might be happening, and I guess I couldn't blame him for that. He didn't like it when I got involved in cases, and I seemed to be unable to stop myself when something interesting was happening—like an emergency. It was no wonder he'd told me to stay put.

But now, I felt like I must have been forgotten. I bent down to reach for my purse, deciding it was time to go. I would leave the papers here in Mitch's office. I'd already explained everything to him, and I was sure he'd want to look through the folders. They would be safer here at the police station than at my house, and I was sure that Mitch would be livid if I tried to take them out with me again.

But just as I stood, the door to Mitch's office burst open again. Mitch looked pale and angry, and he was shouting something into his radio. He saw me standing and pointed at the seat to indicate I should sit down again.

I sat down, looking uneasily at Mitch as he listened to the squawking voice of an officer coming over his radio.

"No sir," the voice said. "We haven't heard anything from either of them recently. We had an officer close to Alice's house, but he confirmed that Alice isn't there right now. He searched the premises completely and said she's definitely not home. We've got someone on the way to Sydney's house as we speak, and they should be able to report back in a few minutes."

"Good, keep me updated on Sydney," Mitch said into the radio, his voice agitated and loud. "Now where else could Alice be? Send someone to search her café right away! And report back to me on Sydney. We have to find them both, and soon."

"Roger that. We'll keep you posted."

Mitch finally looked over at me, and I looked back at him with wide eyes. "What was that all about?" I asked, almost afraid of the answer I would get.

"Well, I don't think Norman is the killer," Mitch said blankly.

I furrowed my brow. "What do you mean?"

My heart had started pounding again. Whatever had just happened must have truly been an emergency. Mitch did not look happy, and I was feeling quite worried at the fact that he seemed so eager to find out the locations of both Sydney and Alice. Why would he be so desperate to find them?

Mitch let out a long, frustrated sigh. "Norman was just found dead behind the Sunshine Springs Liquor Store." Mitch's voice sounded far too calm for the news he had just delivered.

I looked up at him, feeling even more shocked. "What?!?"

Mitch nodded sadly. "The mayor is dead," he confirmed. "Which puts a bit of a wrench in your theory that he was the one who killed Trevor. I've got my officers searching frantically for both Sydney and Alice as we speak."

"Why Alice?" I asked angrily. "She didn't commit this murder!"

Mitch gave me a long-suffering look. "Izzy, let's be real. I hope she didn't commit the murder, and I still have a hard time believing that she would have done that. But there *is* evidence against her, and we have a killer on the loose. I need to find her and make sure there's no more evidence against her. Not only that, but I need to find her because if she is indeed not the killer, then it's quite possible that whoever is doing this is after her next. They seem to be interested in killing off people associated with this case, and Alice is definitely associated with this case."

I felt all of the blood in my veins turn to ice.

Until that moment, I hadn't considered the possibility that Alice might be in danger herself. But Mitch was right: if someone had killed Norman, what was to stop them from killing Alice, too?

I tried to comfort myself with the thought that at least Alice didn't know anything about the election fraud, so perhaps if the killer was after people involved with the fraud, then Alice would be spared. But this small glimmer of hope didn't do much to stop the fear that continued to rush through me.

I jumped to my feet. "We have to get Alice!"

But as I turned toward the door, Mitch's voice stopped me.

"No, *we* don't have to get Alice. *I* have to get Alice. You need to go home and stay out of the way. I don't want you getting caught up in this and ending up hurt or dead."

I spun around and looked at Mitch with fire in my eyes. Sometimes I tried to appease him when he told me to leave things alone, but this was not one of those times. Right now, all I could think of was Alice and the fact that someone might be tracking her down with the intent to kill her.

"Listen, Mitch! Alice is a good friend of mine. She's a good person, and a pillar of this community. I know you're just doing your job and that you have to follow all leads. But I also know in my heart that she's not guilty. If anything happens to her and I could have helped her, I will never forgive myself. I'm going to her café to look for her, and you can't stop me."

Mitch gave me a pleading look. He must have realized that I didn't intend to back down on this. "Izzy, this is a dangerous situation. And even if you do find Alice, what are you going to do that my officers can't? It's better for you to stay out of it."

Tears sprung to my eyes. I knew that he was technically right, but I couldn't bring myself to sit this out. How could I go home and wait, knowing that Alice might be out there in trouble?

Mitch gave me a long, resigned sigh. "Okay, fine. I can't believe I'm saying this, but why don't you come with me in my squad car. If you're going to insist on running around looking for Alice, I'd rather you did it with me so that I can keep an eye on you and keep you safe."

I grinned. "Thank you! I promise I'll be good!"

Mitch grunted. "You've broken promises like that more times than I can count. But come on. We don't have time to waste arguing about this."

A few minutes later, I was riding with Mitch in his squad car as he headed toward Alice's café with his lights flashing and sirens blaring. When we got to the café, there were already several police officers surrounding it. I heard a woman screaming hysterically, and I instinctively reached to open the door and jump out of the car. Was that Alice? Had she been hurt? Was I too late to help her?

But Mitch's stern voice stopped me before I could take off toward the screaming. "Izzy, stay with me. We don't know what's going on over there, and it might be dangerous."

Reluctantly, I nodded and fell into step behind him as he cautiously approached the scene with his hand on his gun holster. I wanted nothing more than to run forward and find Alice, but I had promised to be good. I was going to do my best to keep that promise.

As we approached the scene, however, I quickly saw that it wasn't Alice causing the commotion. Instead, I saw Sydney. She was screaming hysterically and dashing around trying to launch punches at Mitch's officers, who were desperately trying to calm her down.

"It wasn't me! I didn't kill Trevor. It was Alice, and you need to find her! Now she's killed Norman, too."

"Uh-oh," Mitch said. "Looks like she's already heard the news about her secret boyfriend's death."

Mitch rushed forward to help his officers talk to Sydney, but I held back. I had a feeling that the sight of me would only make Sydney angrier. Besides, I wasn't that interested in talking to her. At best, she had been involved in some sort of conspiracy to defraud the people of Sunshine Springs into voting for Norman. And at worst, she was involved in a murder scheme that had now extended to her boyfriend.

I wasn't sure I believed that she would murder Norman. She had seemed to care about him quite a bit when I saw them together at the winery. But had that all been an act? Had she been playing a part so that Norman wouldn't suspect her, and then had she killed him, too? Or maybe she somehow found out that Norman had indeed been the one who killed Trevor, and she had reacted in a fit of anger. Had Norman threatened to expose her part in the election scandal, and had she panicked? The possibilities seemed endless.

Of course, I knew that Mitch would be saying that another possibility was that Alice had killed both Trevor and Norman. From an objective standpoint, I supposed one could look at things that way. But I still couldn't bring myself to believe that Alice would do something like that. It just wasn't possible. Not the Alice I knew. Not the sweet owner of the Morning Brew café.

With a heavy heart, I walked around the corner of Alice's café and peeked inside. Everything inside was dark, but I peered through all the available windows and tried to see whether anything looked amiss. Nothing was moving inside, and all of the tables and chairs appeared to be in their normal positions, with the chairs flipped upside down on the tables as they were every night when Alice closed.

I considered the possibility that Alice could be hiding somewhere in the back room, and I tried not to think about why she would hide if the police were after her. She couldn't be guilty. She just couldn't. If she was hiding, it was only because she was scared out of her wits. And who could blame her for that? I'd be scared too if half the Sunshine Springs Police Department came knocking at my door, even if I was innocent.

As I was peering into one of the side windows, I suddenly saw the front door open. Mitch's officers must have figured out a way inside. I peered excitedly over, hoping that meant that Alice had arrived and opened the door for them. But I still didn't see her anywhere. It was more likely that one of the officers had picked the lock.

I watched as two officers rushed into the café with their flashlight beams sweeping back and forth across the dark room. Even with the light from the flashlights illuminating the café, nothing seemed amiss. I watched the officers go into the back room, and I wasn't sure whether I was hoping Alice would be there or not. When they came back to the front, though, they were alone. I let out a sigh, whether of relief or frustration I wasn't sure. Alice wasn't here.

I walked back around to the front of the building, where Mitch now had Sydney somewhat subdued. She wasn't in handcuffs, but she had calmed down significantly. Two of Mitch's officers held her arms firmly on each side, as if to warn her that she better not try to run away.

Even though she wasn't trying to get away anymore, she was still ranting at Mitch about how this was all Alice's doing. Hearing her words, I could no longer hold in my anger. I rushed up and pointed a finger at her. "It wasn't Alice! It was you! Alice wouldn't hurt anyone, and you know that. You're the one who was involved in all sorts of shady things like trying to rig the election for Norman."

"Get her away from me!" Sydney screamed, and Mitch gave me a warning look telling me that I wasn't helping things.

I felt a little bit guilty, but only a little bit. My anger was so great in that moment that I couldn't resist one more dig at her. "I found the evidence that you were committing election fraud. It's in Mitch's office right now!"

Sydney's face drained of color, which I almost found amusing. How long had she thought she could keep up that ruse? Perhaps she'd thought that since Trevor was dead and Norman had promised to destroy the papers that no one would ever find out about what she'd done. She was oh so wrong about that. I thought about yelling at her some more, but instead I turned to Mitch.

"Aren't you going to arrest her? She was involved in election fraud, and I bet she had something to do with Norman's and Trevor's murders."

"How dare you!" Sydney yelled. "I would never have hurt Norman. And as much as I didn't like Trevor, I never would have killed him."

"All right, Izzy," Mitch said. "That's enough. Let me handle this."

He turned back toward Sydney. "I do find it hard to believe that you would have committed murder, and it's true that we don't have any evidence against you for the actual murders. But what we do have is plenty of evidence that you were involved with election fraud here in Sunshine Springs, which is a very serious crime. And for that reason, I'm placing you under arrest. Sydney Joyner, you have the right to remain silent. Anything you say can and will be used against you in a court of law. You have the right to an attorney. If you cannot afford an attorney, one will be appointed for you...."

Sydney started screaming as Mitch attempted to continue reciting her rights to her. "I didn't do anything! Izzy is telling lies about me! I'm completely innocent!"

I turned away. I didn't want to hear any more of this. Mitch's officers would take Sydney down to the station, where she would give a statement and probably be released on bail. But at the end of it all, I wasn't so concerned with Sydney and what happened to her. I agreed with Mitch that the evidence that she was the murderer wasn't that strong. But if she wasn't, then who was? And was the murderer after Alice right now?

I shivered, wondering if Alice would be the next body to turn up, but I pushed the thought away. I couldn't let myself think like that. I also couldn't let myself wonder if the reason Alice had gone missing was that she had indeed become the next victim of the murderer.

I walked back to Mitch's car and waited for him there, trying the whole time to figure out where else Alice might have gone. I pulled out my phone and sent her a text.

Where are you? I'm worried about you. Please, let me know you're okay.

Several minutes later, when Mitch finally came back to the squad car and sat in the driver's seat without a word, Alice still hadn't texted me back.

"Any idea where else Alice might be?" Mitch asked after a short silence.

I stared down at my phone, which still had no new messages, and shook my head sadly.

"I have no idea. I wish I knew, but her whole life was at her café. If she's not there and she's not at her house, I honestly don't know where she could be. If it was during the daytime, I'd say she was at Sophia's Snips. But obviously Sophia's is closed right now, so I don't know where else to look."

Mitch nodded grimly, and started speaking into his radio, telling his officers to search throughout Sunshine Springs and let him know immediately if they found Alice. I remained silent for the rest of the ride back to the station, lost in my troubled thoughts. After he parked, Mitch asked me if I wanted to come in and give a statement about how I'd found the official election fraud documents, but I begged off and told him I would come in the morning. For now, I was too tired and too worried about Alice to think clearly enough to give a statement.

Mitch understood and let me go. But even once I'd made it home and collapsed into bed, I couldn't find sleep for my exhausted mind. I tossed and turned for a long time, trying to think of where Alice might be and of what I could do to solve the case now that Norman was dead. It was a long time before I finally fell asleep, and my dreams were filled with even more worried and troubled thoughts.

Whatever the morning brought, I knew that the next few days were going to be tough.

CHAPTER FIFTEEN

The next morning, I went to the police station and gave a statement regarding what I knew about the election fraud scandal. Mitch was in a foul mood, and I couldn't blame him: while I was at the station, I learned that Alice was still missing. This didn't surprise me much, since I still hadn't received a text message back from her. But it was still frustrating to hear. She wasn't doing herself any favors by hiding out, and I had to believe that the reason she was missing was that she was hiding out. I couldn't stand the thought of it being anything else—like her being dead somewhere at the hand of the murderer who was still on the loose.

Sydney had been charged with election fraud, and she was currently out on bail. I heard Mitch telling another officer that she'd agreed to cooperate with the investigation in exchange for a lighter sentence, but it didn't sound like there was any evidence against her that she had murdered anyone. Still, I knew Mitch was keeping a close eye on her since she was so closely connected to this case.

Feeling frustrated, I went by the Drunken Pie Café to check on things. Tiffany was there and in a good mood, and she told me she had no problem running the café by herself for the rest of the day. She wanted the extra hours because she was trying to save extra money for Christmas gifts. She also mentioned to me that Scott had come by and bought a whole strawberry moonshine pie.

"The whole pie?" I mused. "That's interesting. He usually just takes the free slices I offer him."

"I know," Tiffany said. "But he was adamant that he needed a whole pie, and he was frantic that we might not have one. He said he meant to special order one and forgot, but he got here right when we opened to be sure he got one."

"Weird," I said. I wondered if the fact that Scott had purchased an entire strawberry moonshine pie, which happened to be one of Molly's favorites, had anything to do with the possibility that he might propose today. I made a mental note to text Molly and ask what she was doing tonight, although of course I wouldn't say anything about the pie. If Scott was proposing, I didn't want to ruin his surprise. And I also wasn't going to say anything to Tiffany, because I knew Molly was trying to keep things quiet about the proposal until it actually happened. I didn't know how successful she'd been at that since Grams said everyone at Sophia's Snips had been talking about the fact that Scott was about to propose, but I at least was going to do my part to keep things quiet.

After checking on a few more things at the café, I left the place in Tiffany's capable hands. I was dying to know whether Mitch had found any news on Alice, but I refrained from actually calling him. I knew he was busy, and that I was getting on his nerves by getting so involved in everything. But I still hadn't heard anything back from Alice, which made me think that she hadn't been found. If she had been, she would have texted or called me.

Unless of course she'd been arrested and didn't have access to her phone.

I pushed that thought away, and tried to think of what I could do to keep myself from going crazy with all of the different worries I had over this murder case. After mulling over options for a few moments, I decided to leave Sprinkles with Grams and then head to the winery to hash things out with Theo. I texted Molly to see if she wanted to join, but she didn't answer me. Maybe she was really busy at the library.

I frowned at my phone. I wasn't having much luck contacting anyone, but hopefully Theo would be around. Even better would be if he'd heard any updates from Mitch, since he and Mitch often talked to each other about whatever cases Mitch was working on. Theo could never resist passing on the updates to me that he'd heard from Mitch.

Half an hour later, I made it to the winery, where I was surprised to see not only Theo, but Scott as well.

"Scott!" I greeted him. "Good to see you. You haven't been by the café for a while with any deliveries, although I heard you came in this morning and ordered a pie."

Scott looked around nervously, as though he had just been caught in the middle of some sort of untoward activity.

"Yes, well, I always want to support your business." He laughed nervously. "Anyway, thanks for your help, Theo. And Izzy, good to see you—but I have to get going. I have a lot to do today."

With that, he made a mad dash for the door, leaving me alone with Theo in the tasting room. There weren't even any winery employees there. Technically the tasting room wasn't open yet, even though the front door was unlocked. Most tourists wouldn't be stopping by this early, so Theo probably didn't worry about anyone wandering in.

"What's wrong with Scott?" I asked. "I've never seen him look quite so frazzled."

"He did seem a bit on edge, didn't he?" Theo said. "But he didn't mention anything that might have been wrong. He was just in here doing a special order for a couple bottles of wine."

I raised an eyebrow. "A special order? I wonder if this has anything to do with the possibility that he might propose to Molly."

At that, Theo laughed and winked at me. "I wouldn't know anything about that."

I couldn't resist pushing for a little more information. "Oh, come on! What do you know? I won't tell Molly! I promise!"

Theo rolled his eyes at me. "I don't trust you not to tell her. You're her best friend. My lips are sealed, and that's that."

I could tell from the stubborn look in his eyes that he was serious. I made a pouty face at him, then asked, "Are your lips also sealed about Trevor's murder case? I suppose you heard that Norman was also killed last night?"

"I heard. The whole town is buzzing with the news by now. But if you're asking whether I know more about the case than you do, then the answer to that is probably no. I had coffee with Mitch this morning at your café, but he didn't have much to report."

I frowned. "You actually came into the café when I wasn't there? Why don't you ever come when I'm working?"

Theo laughed. "Are you ever working these days? Seems like you're always running around looking for leads on a murder case."

"Hey! I work a lot! Tiffany is only part time, so I pick up the rest of the slack. Besides, I've worked so hard for so long at that café that you can't blame me for taking a few days off now and then, can you?"

Theo shrugged. "I guess not. But anyway, Mitch didn't have much to tell me. He said Sydney had a solid alibi for both murders. In Norman's case, a pizza delivery guy verified that he delivered a pizza to her house, and she was home during the time that Norman would have been at the liquor store. She actually has security cameras at her place, and Mitch checked them. The only time she opened the door to the house was when the pizza delivery guy came. There's no way she's the one who killed Norman."

"What about Trevor? Is there any possibility she killed him? Surely since she was on the elections committee Mitch can't overlook the fact that she would have had a motive to kill Trevor."

Theo shook his head. "Mitch checked into that, but Sydney was seen by several people inside the library building during the whole time frame that would fit the time of death for Trevor. She's not the murderer. I hate to say it, but there don't seem to be many options other than Alice at this point."

"There has to be someone else," I said, feeling a familiar sense of dread rising within me. I couldn't betray Alice by allowing myself to think that she was guilty. "What about someone else who might have been connected to the election fraud case?" I furrowed my brow, trying to think. "What about Cody? I know Mitch said he had an alibi, but is the alibi solid? Cody seems like he might have had motive to kill off people involved."

But Theo was shaking his head. "I actually asked Mitch about that, because you're right: the fact that Cody seemed to have known about all of this election fraud makes him look suspicious. But Mitch told me that several teenagers who were working one of the food tables at the event at the library confirmed that Cody was speaking with them during the whole timeframe of Trevor's death. And it wasn't just one witness who might have been mistaken about the time. It was three or four different witnesses. Cody's got a rock solid alibi."

"Darn," I said. "Another lead that's a dead-end. There must be something we're missing, though. Who else might have been involved in this?"

Theo shrugged. "That's the question Mitch has been asking himself for the last several days, but last night didn't make things any clearer. Even knowing about the election fraud doesn't widen the circle of possible suspects. According to Sydney, she and Norman were working alone. Mitch also told me that he brought Cody in for questioning about the election fraud this morning, because he was worried that Cody might have been the one that killed Norman. But Cody had an alibi for last night as well. He was out with some friends at one of the restaurants on Main Street. Cody did talk to Mitch about the election fraud, though. As far as he knew, Sydney and Norman were the only ones involved."

"Why in the world didn't he go to the police in the first place if he knew about the fraud?"

Theo shrugged. "Cody told Mitch that he and Trevor knew about the election fraud and were planning to go to the police, but that they wanted to get their evidence organized first."

I made a face. "Organized? That seems a little strange. The papers and folders that I saw seemed pretty organized to me."

"I'm just telling you what Mitch told me," Theo said. "According to Cody, he and Trevor were working on gathering and organizing evidence when Trevor died. After that, Cody said the evidence suddenly went missing from his office, which fits with what you said about how you saw Norman sneaking in to steal it. Cody said that when he realized the evidence was missing, he got scared and thought that maybe the murderer had stolen it. He was worried that if he made a big fuss about it, the murderer might come after him."

I frowned. "I guess that seems plausible."

"Mitch thought so, too. But even Cody said that now that Norman's dead, he has no idea who's behind all of this. He would have said Sydney, but, like I said, Sydney has a solid alibi. Cody suggested Alice again, although he can't explain how she would have been involved in the election fraud scandal."

"There's just no way Alice did this," I said for what felt like the millionth time. "I can't see Alice committing not just one but *two* murders!"

"I agree with you," Theo said. "But even Mitch has to admit that the suspect list has grown quite small. Alice is the only one left that has evidence against her and doesn't have an alibi. And it doesn't help things that she's still missing."

I let out a long sigh. "I'm so frustrated. Alice trusted me to solve this case, and I feel like I've gotten nowhere."

"I wouldn't say you've gotten nowhere," Theo said kindly. "You did uncover the whole election fraud thing."

"I guess," I said sullenly. "But that would have been uncovered eventually, anyway. Whoever it was that killed Norman would have done that regardless of whether or not I was involved. And after Norman's death, his office would've been searched. Mitch would have found that information even without my help."

"True, but he wouldn't have found it quite as soon."

I shrugged. "Big deal. He might have found it a day later—maybe not even that long."

To my surprise, Theo got a silly grin on his face at that moment.

I glared at him. "It's not funny."

"I know. But I was just thinking…if you're feeling so frustrated, why don't you place a special order for wine? That seems to be what everyone else is doing these days. You can chase away your troubles with a glass of delicious pinot from Sunshine Springs Winery." Theo held up a bottle of wine and gave me a smile clearly intended to be an overly-exaggerated salesman's smile.

I groaned at him. "You're incorrigible."

He laughed. "What? That seems to be how Cody is coping with all the stress."

I rolled my eyes. "I'm not sure that I want to emulate Cody Stringer. Besides, I already place enough special orders for wine. I'm always ordering cases for my café."

Theo shrugged. "True enough. But you can never have enough wine. In fact, do you want a complimentary glass right now?"

I widened my eyes at him. "It's not even ten A.M. yet!"

He shrugged again. "So? You don't judge people who order boozy pies before noon at your café, and I don't judge people who order glasses of wine first thing in the morning. What's the difference?"

I just shook my head at him again. "Thanks for the offer, but I really need to get going. I have to see if I can figure out what to do to help find Alice. There must be somewhere she could be hiding that I'm not thinking of!"

"Suit yourself," Theo said. "Swing by later if you get bored. I'll be working the front counter all day because one of my employees called in sick."

"I'll keep it in mind."

"You do that," Theo said. "I'd love the chance to talk to someone intelligent. I can't stand all the vapid conversations I have to have with these tourists every time I work the tasting room."

"I'll think about it," I promised. "For now, I need to work on this case."

I bid Theo goodbye and left the winery, but my mood was even worse than before. Usually, speaking with Theo made me feel better. But today, I just felt more frustrated—a frustration I was sure that even a special order of wine from Theo wasn't going to cure.

Only finding Alice would make me feel better.

But thinking of the special orders of wine made me think of Cody. I couldn't shake the feeling that it was strange that he and Trevor had waited to tell the police about the election fraud. If they knew about it, why hold back? From what I had seen in the folders I took, Trevor had already had plenty of evidence. He hadn't needed any more to prove his case, so why had he been waiting? Something did not add up here.

I decided then and there that I was going to pay a visit to Cody and see what else he might know. He'd been hiding the election fraud from the police for a reason. Was it possible he was hiding more clues?

I couldn't be sure, but I had a feeling that if I went and talked to Cody, I might find a new lead, so that's exactly what I was going to do. I sped toward Sunshine Springs, and toward the building where Cody's office was located. This time, I knew for sure that I wouldn't run into Norman sneaking around. But I hoped that I *would* run into Cody Stringer—and that he would have some answers for me.

CHAPTER SIXTEEN

When I arrived at Cody's office, he was indeed there. But he wasn't in the mood to talk, and he didn't look like he was planning to actually be in that office much longer. The room was full of cardboard boxes, which he was rapidly packing up with all of his belongings from the office.

I rapped on the door a bit timidly. "Cody? I was wondering if you might have a moment to talk."

Cody looked up at me and glared, his eyes narrowing into slits that looked downright creepy. "I'm not interested in talking, especially not to you. I know you're trying to solve this murder case, but I've already given all my statements to the police. If they won't tell you what I said, then that's your problem. I'm not going over everything again."

He turned his back on me in a huff and continued to pack. For a few moments, I watched him in silence, trying to figure out what to say. He was right: I couldn't make him talk to me. And I was sure he knew that the police weren't going to tell me anything. But I wasn't giving up. I decided to try to get him to loosen up with a little bit of small talk.

"Moving offices, huh?"

As soon as I said the words, I regretted them. Cody looked up at me with such an angry expression that I felt a chill run down my spine. I'd thought that it was a relatively benign comment. Moving offices didn't seem to be that surprising of an occurrence, since his boss had been dead for a few days. But Cody apparently wasn't in the mood to talk about the move.

"Good job, Captain Obvious. Yes, I'm moving offices. In fact, I'm moving out of town completely. I've had enough of this place."

My eyes widened slightly. "You're moving out of Sunshine Springs?"

I didn't bother to hide the surprise in my voice. Yes, he'd been through a lot here in the last few days. But it was relatively rare for a local to move. Folks who'd been born and raised here just couldn't imagine living anywhere else. But, if anything could drive someone away from our little town, I supposed that having your boss murdered in cold blood would do it.

"Where will you go?" I choked out. "And don't you want to know what happens with the investigation into Trevor's murder?"

Cody gave me a disgusted laugh. "I'm sure I'll hear what happens, but I'm not sticking around to wait for the news. This town is a mess, and the police are a joke. We've had two murders in the last week and they still haven't arrested Alice! It's clear she's guilty and they're just letting her run free."

I bit my lip. I had a feeling Cody was baiting me. If he knew I was investigating the case, he'd probably heard that I was trying to prove Alice's innocence. I didn't want to give him the satisfaction of getting a rise out of me, and so I kept my mouth shut.

But Cody barely noticed my silence, and a few seconds later he continued with his rant. "Besides, there's no work for me here. As of right now, there's not anyone running for mayor. And tell me, would you want to work as a campaign manager in a town where all of the candidates for mayor keep turning up dead?"

I shrugged. I guess he had a point there.

He still didn't seem interested in talking to me about the details of the case, but I figured that while I was there I might as well press him to see if he had anything to tell me. If he truly was leaving town, this might be my last chance. So when he looked at me with an annoyed glare and bellowed out, "Is there anything else, or can I get back to packing now," I took a deep breath and decided to go for it.

"I was just wondering if you knew of any other shady activities that Norman might have been involved in. You knew about the election fraud. Is it possible there were any other clues in this case that you might be able to remember?"

I intentionally refrained from accusing him of holding back clues on purpose, even though that's what I really wanted to do. But he must have known that's what I was implying, because he completely blew up at me after that.

"I have nothing else to say about any of this. Like I said, I've given my statement to the police, and I don't have to tell you anything. If you have questions about the case, you should go talk to them. In the meantime, I'm getting out of Sunshine Springs as soon as possible. I should have left years ago. I'm too good for this place. Now, if you don't mind, I'd appreciate it if you'd leave so I can finish packing."

I decided that it was probably best to take his advice and get out of there. He obviously wasn't going to share any more information with me, and I didn't have time to waste. I needed to figure out what else I could do to find Alice and solve this case. I walked out of his office without another word, and he didn't look back at me or say goodbye.

I felt dejected as I walked down the hallway. I still couldn't shake the idea that Cody knew more than he was letting on, but how was I supposed to figure out what he knew when he wouldn't talk and was leaving town? Even if I'd been willing to sneak into Cody's office and go through his stuff, risking Mitch's wrath or a charge of trespassing, that wasn't an option since he was packing up and leaving. I had reached quite an impasse.

I glanced back at Cody one last time. Perhaps he was right. Perhaps he was too "good" for this town. His snobby attitude wasn't a good fit for a place like Sunshine Springs. As I looked at him now, I noticed that his clothes were quite expensive-looking. When I thought about it, I realized that he was always dressed quite fancily. I hadn't thought that campaign managers made that much money, but come to think of it, I didn't actually know that much about what campaign managers were paid. I didn't know that much about Cody, either. He didn't have any other family here in Sunshine Springs, but perhaps he had family somewhere else that had money.

In any case, his moving away would be no great loss to Sunshine Springs. I did think it was odd, however, that he was moving in the middle of the murder investigation. If it hadn't been for the fact that Mitch and Theo had both told me that Cody had a strong alibi for Trevor's and Norman's murders, I would have been quite suspicious of him. As it was, I couldn't shake the feeling that he knew more than he was letting on.

But no matter how strong that feeling was, if I couldn't convince him to talk, and I couldn't convince Mitch to continue investigating Cody further, what good did that feeling do me? I couldn't think of any other way to find out what Cody knew.

I looked at my phone, willing it to buzz with a message from Alice. But she still hadn't contacted me, and with every hour that passed, I became more worried that something was truly wrong. Had the murderer found her? I couldn't bear to think about it, and yet I couldn't get the thought out of my head. As I looked down at my phone, it suddenly buzzed, nearly causing me to shriek. When I calmed down and looked, I saw that it was Molly calling.

I smiled, despite everything that was going on. It was always good to hear from my best friend.

"What's up, Molly?" I said into the phone.

"Izzy! I'm so glad you answered. Are you working at the café today?"

"No," I said, and then hesitated before saying anything else. I hoped Molly wasn't going to give me a hard time about the fact that I was investigating this case. I was already trying to come up with an excuse as to why I needed to keep sleuthing as I said, "I took the day off to get some stuff done."

Even though I didn't elaborate, I was sure Molly knew what that "stuff" was. But Molly didn't seem interested in reprimanding me for sleuthing right now. Instead, she let out a long sigh of relief. "Oh, thank goodness you're not working! I need your help. It's an emergency!"

"What's wrong?" I asked, feeling slightly confused. Molly did sound a bit agitated, but she didn't sound like she was in the middle of an emergency. I hoped she was just being dramatic and that nothing was truly wrong. I wasn't sure I could handle any more deaths this week.

"I need to find a new outfit for tonight!"

I relaxed, and almost laughed. "That's your definition of an emergency?" I teased.

Molly huffed into the phone. "It's not funny! It is an emergency! I think Scott might propose to me tonight. If tonight's the night, then I want to look perfect, but I have nothing to wear! Please, can you come shopping with me and help me find something?"

I highly doubted that Molly had nothing to wear. She was usually quite put-together and had her own easy sense of style. But I understood that she wanted something extra special for tonight. It's not every day that a girl had the love of her life ask her to marry him.

"You do know that I have no fashion sense, right?" I asked. It was true. I had never been able to effortlessly put together an outfit like Molly could. I tried to stick with classic looks for the most part, which was funny considering how eccentrically my grandmother dressed. Grams and I were on pretty much opposite ends of the fashion spectrum. But even though Molly knew that, she didn't seem to care.

"You're wrong, Izzy! You do have some fashion sense. Besides, I just need someone to come with me for moral support. This might be one of the biggest nights of my life, and I want to look good. You're my best friend, so it's your duty to help me out with this!"

I chuckled. "Okay, fine. I'll help you out. You want to go shopping downtown on Main Street? We could meet at my café and fuel up with pie and coffee before heading out. Or even pie and wine! Your choice."

Even though I couldn't see Molly, I could tell from the tone in her voice that she was grinning. "That sounds perfect. I owe you one."

"Don't mention it. I'll see you in a few."

As I ended the call, I couldn't help but smile. It would be good to be around my best friend for a while. Maybe focusing on something besides the case would help clear my mind. Besides, this was important to Molly, and therefore it was important to me. I wanted to be there for my friend.

I texted Grams to ask her if she could keep watching Sprinkles a little bit longer, and she happily agreed. Then I started heading toward the Drunken Pie Café, doing my best to push thoughts of Cody and of Norman's and

Trevor's murders out of my mind.

But that was easier said than done. Even as I walked into my café and greeted Molly, I couldn't stop wondering where Alice was, and whether I had already run out of time to save her.

CHAPTER SEVENTEEN

If I thought that I could escape thinking about the case while walking around Main Street in Sunshine Springs, I had been sorely mistaken. When we walked into the first boutique, the teen sales girl recognized me immediately and let out a squeal.

"Isabelle James, right?" she asked.

I nodded, feeling suddenly self-conscious and wondering why this teenager was so excited to see me. "Yes. But, call me Izzy. No one calls me Isabelle except my grandmother when she's angry with me."

The girl laughed. "Okay, Izzy it is. It's a beautiful name! I can't believe you're here. You're the talk of the town right now!"

"I am?" I asked, feeling a bit of panic rising in the pit of my stomach. I tried to think of why I might be the focus of the Sunshine Springs gossip mill, and I didn't like the answer I came up with.

The girl nodded vigorously. "Yes, everyone's talking about how you're trying to solve this murder case and figure out who killed Norman and Trevor! I can't believe we've had two murders in one week! Are you getting any closer to figuring out what happened?"

I wanted to groan, but managed to keep a pleasant look on my face. So much for escaping from the case for a while: apparently it was going to follow me everywhere I went, and apparently everyone in town knew that I was doing detective work again.

"There isn't much to tell," I said to the girl. "To be honest, I thought that Norman was the murderer until he turned up dead himself, which means I now feel like I'm back at square one. But I'll keep trying. What else can I do?"

I shrugged, and hoped that would be the end of it. But the girl didn't seem interested in letting the subject drop.

"It's just awful, isn't it? I can't believe Alice is missing? It's all anyone in town is talking about. Some people think it's possible that she did it, but that's hard to believe. She's always so sweet and quiet. But maybe she was hiding a scary side of her personality underneath all that sweetness!"

"I don't think it was Alice," I said, trying to keep the annoyance out of my voice. "But don't worry. We'll figure out who did this and make sure that Sunshine Springs is safe again."

"We're so lucky to have you on the case!" the girl gushed again.

Molly gave me a sympathetic look, but then escaped into the fitting rooms with a little wave. I glared after her, wanting to ask her how she could abandon me to this girl's questioning. But Molly shut the fitting room door behind her without turning around again. I knew that was purposeful. She didn't want to discuss this case any more than I did right now. Molly was focused on a potential proposal, and why wouldn't she be? Surely, that was much more exciting than rehashing the same thing over and over on a murder case that seemed to be nothing but dead ends.

But the teenage sales clerk was happy to rehash things. She looked at me with wide eyes. "I heard that Cody Stringer is really upset about all of this. My boyfriend told me that Cody is so distraught that he's talking about leaving town!"

I looked at the girl with mild interest. "Your boyfriend knows Cody? Was he interning for Trevor's campaign office?"

It seemed a little odd that a teenage boy would be hanging out with a character like Cody Stringer, but perhaps campaign internships were a popular part-time job for high-schoolers.

But the girl shook her head. "Oh, no. But my boyfriend plays football for Sunshine Springs High, and Cody works as a volunteer coach for the football program. That's how they know each other."

"Really?" I raised an eyebrow. This was news to me, and quite surprising. Cody didn't seem like the type who would enjoy working with teenagers. He struck me as a sullen person who was quite full of himself, so why would he enjoy working with a bunch of teenagers who were also quite sullen and full of themselves? That didn't seem like a good combination.

But the girl was nodding enthusiastically. "Oh, yes! Cody's a really good guy, and surprisingly funny. He has such a great heart, too. He's always so nice to all the boys, and does whatever he can to help them improve their football game. He would hang out with them after practice, and seemed like the kind of guy who would just be there for you. It's such a loss that he's planning to move away from Sunshine Springs. He has such a heart of gold."

Molly stepped out of the fitting room as the girl was saying this, and she raised an eyebrow at me. I nearly choked, and wasn't sure what to say. True, I didn't know Cody that well, but I never would have described him as someone with a heart of gold. From the look on Molly's face, she was thinking the same thing.

I was more convinced than ever that Cody was up to something. He seemed like such a shady character, and I felt like there must have been a reason he was hanging out with all these high-schoolers—a reason beyond the fact that he wanted to give back to his community. He'd made it quite clear in his office earlier that he was not a fan of this community, so why would he volunteer to help its teenagers?

I didn't say any of this to the girl, of course. Instead, I looked at Molly and tried to focus on helping her with her shopping. Right now, she was wearing a red sweater dress. The dress hugged her curves in all the right places, and the color looked fantastic against her skin. It brightened up her eyes and hair, and although my friend always looked beautiful, I couldn't help thinking that she looked especially beautiful right now.

"Oh my goodness!" I exclaimed. "You have to get that dress! Scott will die of delight when he sees you in it."

Molly grinned and bit her lower lip nervously. "You really think so?"

"I know so!" I replied. "That dress was made for you."

Apparently, the teenage sales clerk agreed. She clapped her hands and squealed. "Oh, you look amazing. Just pair the dress with some black tights or leggings and a pair of knee-high black leather boots! Scott's going to propose tonight for sure!"

Molly and I both looked at the girl with questioning glances. Neither of us had actually said anything about Scott proposing since we came into the store. The girl seemed to realize this from the way we looked at her, and she shrugged. "What? It's not like the whole town doesn't already know that Scott's on the verge of proposing. Everyone is just waiting for the news."

Molly sighed, but then giggled. "I guess no one can keep a secret around here. I'll go ahead and change, and then see if there are any black boots for sale here that I like."

She disappeared back into the dressing room, and, surprisingly, the teenage girl was quiet for a few moments. That quiet gave me a few moments to think, and I thought about how it was all too true what Molly had said: nobody could keep a secret around here.

Did this girl's boyfriend know some of Cody's secrets? And, if so, would he be willing to share them with me?

I glanced over at the girl. "What's your boyfriend's name? Would I recognize him from the football team?"

"Oh, yes!" She gushed. "His name is Sammy Jenkins. He's the starting quarterback. I'm so lucky that he's my boyfriend. He's the best catch at the high school, and you'd think that he would go for one of the cheerleaders and not an artsy type like me. But he knows what he wants, and it's not one of those ditzy pom-pom girls."

The girl beamed at me proudly, and I smiled back at her. On another day, I might have tried to explain to her that in a few years, no one would care who had been the quarterback and who had been one of the "pom-pom girls" or not. But right now, I was too focused on other things to worry about trying to give any life lessons.

"He sounds wonderful," I said kindly.

And it sounds like I need to pay him a visit, I thought.

Twenty minutes later, Molly had paid for her new dress and boots, and was giving me a big hug out on the sidewalk. "Thank you so much for your help! I'm going to go home now and get ready for this date. I'll let you know the minute he proposes!"

I smiled. "Okay. But don't be too disappointed if he doesn't propose tonight. You know it's coming soon either way."

"I know. But it's definitely going to be tonight!" She winked at me and gave me another hug, then skipped off down the sidewalk.

I decided to swing by my café and pick up a pie—a non-boozy one, so that I could share it with seventeen-year-old Sammy Jenkins. All kids loved pie, and perhaps teenage boys more than anyone. Maybe if I showed up at his house with a giant double fudge treat, he would be willing to tell me what he knew about Cody.

It was worth a shot. This was the only lead I had right now, and I had to follow it and figure out what I could before Cody left town for good.

Something told me that if I figured out what Cody knew, I'd be able to figure out this murder case—and I'd be able to save Alice.

CHAPTER EIGHTEEN

Sammy Jenkins lived in a nice neighborhood a couple blocks away from Sunshine Springs High. When I rang the doorbell to his house, I was happy that he was the one who answered. He was wearing a gigantic pair of headphones, and he looked annoyed by my interruption.

"My parents aren't home right now," he said. Then he glanced down at the pie box. "Hey, you're the pie lady, aren't you? But I don't think anyone here ordered pie."

I smiled at him in what I hoped was a disarming fashion. "I am indeed the pie lady. I'm Izzy James, the owner of the Drunken Pie Café. I know nobody here ordered pie, and I'm actually not here to see your parents. I'm here to see you, and I brought pie with me because I've never met a high school boy who didn't enjoy pie."

He looked at me doubtfully, as if trying to see what trick I was attempting to pull. I broadened my smile and tried to look convincing. "I promise I don't bite. I just want to ask you a few questions."

Sammy looked back and forth between my face and the pie. He looked conflicted, as though he wanted to let me in so he could eat pie, but he wasn't interested in actually talking to me.

I held the pie box up closer to his face. "You know you want to. It's double chocolate fudge."

He must have been a fan of chocolate, because that convinced him. "Okay, but only for a minute. I'm in the middle of a really great run on my favorite videogame, and once my parents are home they're going to make me stop playing. They're always onto me to get outside and get fresh air, even though I get plenty of fresh air at football practice."

He rolled his eyes, and I refrained from commenting. I agreed with his parents that getting outside and getting fresh air was a better choice than sitting in here staring at the screen, but I wasn't about to tell him that and make him angry at me. Not when I needed his help so badly.

Sammy led me to the kitchen, where I opened the pie box and started cutting him a slice with a plastic pie cutter. When he got a plate from the cupboard and put it in front of me without a word, I put a generous slice of pie on it for him.

Once he had a bite of pie in his mouth, I jumped right in. "The reason I'm here is that I'm wondering whether you can tell me anything about Cody Stringer."

Sammy paused in the middle of chewing and looked up at me with suspicious eyes. He quickly swallowed, and frowned at me. "Look, I don't want any trouble."

I smiled at him reassuringly. "I'm not here to cause you any trouble. But as you may have heard, I'm working on solving the mystery of who murdered Trevor and Norman."

Sammy took another bite of pie and chewed slowly while still eyeing me suspiciously. I waited patiently for him to finish chewing, at which point he said, "I don't know anything about who murdered Trevor or Norman. All I can tell you is that all the gossip I've heard around town says that it was Alice. You know, the lady who owns the Morning Brew Café."

"I know her very well, and I don't believe she murdered Norman and Trevor. I'm following some other leads, and following those clues has led me to believe that Cody Stringer might know something about the case."

I watched Sammy carefully. He looked at me as though expecting me to point a finger at him and accuse him of murder at any second. A thin layer of sweat had broken out on his forehead, and I was feeling pretty confident that I was onto something. Why had he so quickly rushed to say that he didn't want any trouble? And why was he so nervous because of my questions about Cody? He must know something, and I was determined to find out what that something was.

"Has Cody acted strangely over the last few weeks at all? Or has he mentioned anything suspicious that was going on with Trevor or Norman?"

Sammy started sweating even more. He put down his fork and looked back at me nervously. "Look, I don't know anything about the murders, or about what Cody might know about Trevor or Norman. All I know of Cody is that he helps coach the football team. I'm the quarterback, so I see him quite a bit at football practice. But outside of that...it's not like I'm hanging out with him. My impression of him is that he's a good guy, but he's been under a lot of stress lately. Running the campaign for mayor didn't sound like fun, but I don't think that's all that out of the ordinary. Aren't politics always a bit crazy?"

I nodded. "I suppose they are. But Cody never mentioned anything specific about what was stressing him out in the campaign?"

Sammy squirmed uncomfortably in his seat. "I think all of it was stressing him out. But he didn't talk about it much at football practice. He tried to keep things focused on the game."

"Did he mention whether he and Norman were fighting at all?"

Sammy shook his head. "I don't think they were fighting. But, come to think of it, he was fighting with Sydney a lot."

"Sydney Joyner? The elections committee head?"

Sammy shrugged. "I don't know what her exact title is. All I know is that Cody ranted about her now and then. It seemed like there was a lot of bad blood between them, but I couldn't tell you why. Cody hated Sydney. And I mean hated. Just the mention of her name was enough to put him in a bad mood for hours, so we all made sure not to speak of her."

"And you really have no idea why he hated her so much? Did he ever say what she might have done?"

Sammy shook his head. "I have no idea. Like I said, we all tried to avoid the subject. Cody was always lots of fun, except for when Sydney came up. I didn't care what their beef was about, I only cared about having a good time at football practice, and that meant not asking Cody about Sydney."

I frowned, processing all of this information. Again, I wondered if it was possible that Sydney had somehow been the one to kill Trevor and Norman. I had a hard time believing it, considering how much in love she'd seemed to be with Norman when I saw them at the winery. But I told myself that that could have been an act.

Then, another thought hit me: was it possible that the two murders weren't done by the same person? Perhaps Sydney had murdered Trevor, and Cody had murdered Norman. I rubbed my forehead, starting to feel overwhelmed. The further I got into this case, the more complicated it seemed to be.

Sammy was looking at me warily, like he was ready to bolt. I suspected that he knew more about Cody than he was telling me, and I was determined to press him on it. I just had to do it carefully so I didn't push him too far. I didn't want him to shut down completely. But before I could formulate another question, my phone buzzed with an incoming call.

When I looked down at the phone, I saw to my surprise that the caller I.D. had Alice's name on it. With a surprised yelp, I immediately started running for the front door of Sammy's house.

"I gotta go. Thanks for your help, and enjoy the pie."

Unsurprisingly, Sammy didn't beg me to stay. He must have been relieved that I was leaving, but I didn't even bother glancing back to see. As I flew out the front door, I was already pulling my keys out of my purse and running to my car.

"Alice! Where are you! Are you okay? I've been worried sick about you!"

"I'm fine," Alice replied. "I'm sorry I haven't contacted you, but I had my phone turned off, and all the location services turned off. I read on the

Internet how to set up your phone so that nobody could find you, and I didn't want Mitch or anyone bugging me until things with the murder were solved. I didn't want to get arrested."

"Alice," I groaned. "I already told you that the best thing to do is cooperate with Mitch. The more you hide, the more suspicious you look."

"I know," Alice said in a contrite voice. "But I just couldn't stand being a murder suspect. I was also tired of everyone coming into the café looking at me with pity on their faces."

I held back another groan as I started up my car's engine. I was tempted to give Alice a stern talking to, but I refrained for the moment. I figured the best thing I could do right now was to figure out where she was and get to her while she was still in the mood to talk.

"Where are you?" I asked, praying that she would actually tell me.

"I'm hiding out at the high school, in a deserted office in the old sports building."

"Really?" I said as I turned my car toward Sunshine Springs High. It wasn't lost on me that Cody, who was another one of the people tangled up in this case, had connections to Sunshine Springs High as well. Was that just coincidence, or had Alice found something?

When Alice spoke, though, she didn't sound like she'd found anything interesting about the case. "There are people everywhere trying to track me down and accuse me of horrible things I didn't do!"

Alice was speaking in the angriest tone of voice I'd ever heard her use, but I tried to stay calm myself. I had a lot of questions for her, and I was beyond frustrated that she'd disappeared the way she had. But I would save my questions for when I saw her in person. Right now, my priority was getting to her before she could disappear again.

"Okay, tell me exactly where you are. Which building, and which office number? I'm coming to you, and don't worry. I won't let anyone hurt you. But there is a murderer on the loose, and I would feel better if you weren't hiding out on your own where that murderer might find you."

Alice let out what sounded like a resigned sigh, then told me her exact hiding place in the old sports building. I tried to keep her on the phone, thinking that if she kept talking to me she wouldn't be tempted to make a run for it before I got there. But she insisted on hanging up, saying she wanted to turn her phone off again in case someone was tracking it.

I let her go, but immediately called Mitch. He didn't answer his phone, so I called the police station directly. The receptionist told me that Mitch wasn't there at the moment, and asked to take a message. I wasn't about to leave a message with her that I'd found Alice. I didn't want her telling some other officer who would then run out to the high school.

I wanted Mitch. I knew Alice wasn't dangerous, and I knew Mitch would respect Alice. Some of the other officers might rough her up, and I couldn't bear the thought of that. So I merely told the receptionist to let Mitch know that I had an emergency I needed to speak with him about, and that I would appreciate it if he would call me as soon as possible.

I tried Mitch's cell phone again, but he didn't answer. I wished I had a radio so I could page him on the emergency channel, but since I didn't, I left him a voice message telling him where I was going and that I'd found Alice. I knew that as soon as Mitch got the voicemail, he'd hightail it down to the high school.

I just hoped that one or both of us would get there before Alice decided to take off for a new hiding place. My whole body felt like a bundle of nerves as I floored the accelerator in the direction of Sunshine Springs High.

CHAPTER NINETEEN

Before I got to the parking lot outside the old sports building at Sunshine Springs High, I slowed down my driving. I realized that if I came screeching in like a maniac, I might spook Alice and make her bolt before I got to her. I forced myself to park calmly and take a deep breath before getting out of my car.

The November days were short, and it was dark by this point. That darkness only added to the eeriness of the situation. I rushed quickly across the parking lot, trying not to think about how many good hiding spots there were here for a potential murderer. I crept along, wishing more than anything that Sprinkles was with me. Since he wasn't, I could only hope that Mitch would show up soon.

I told myself that I likely wasn't in any real danger. As far as I knew, the only person around the high school right now was Alice. I was the only one who knew she was here, and I doubted that anyone else would have thought to come search for her here. I certainly wouldn't have thought she was here if she hadn't told me.

I continued creeping along until I rounded a corner to see two figures sitting in the middle of the football field. In my hyperaware state, my heart nearly stopped in my throat. But when I realized who the two figures were, I calmed down again and a big grin spread across my face.

Out in the middle of the football field, a picnic blanket had been spread out with several candles glowing around it. Molly and Scott were having a candlelight picnic. I almost laughed out loud, and thought to myself that they were lucky that the temperatures in Sunshine Springs were so mild year round. In many parts of the country, having an outdoor picnic on a November evening would have been impossible.

I smiled as I watched the two of them out there, caught up in their own little world. I recalled Molly telling me once that she and Scott had shared a kiss on the football field in high school. Molly had been embarrassed by it, saying that they'd both been buzzed on cheap wine someone had swiped from their parents' house, and that nothing had been meant by the kiss. And yet, now that I thought about it, I remembered Molly's cheeks turning pink at the memory. Had she been embarrassed, or had she actually thought fondly of that moment? Had thinking back on that long-ago kiss stirred up some sort of suppressed desire?

Whatever the case, it looked like Scott had planned a romantic date for Molly by recreating that kiss. From my vantage point, I could see that he had wine, pie, and a spread of other food set up. There was also a small gift bag. And even from this distance, I could see the wide smiles on both of their faces. I continued smiling myself, feeling quite sure now that Molly was correct in thinking that Scott would propose tonight. I could hardly wait to hear about it.

But right now, I needed to find out where Alice was. Besides, I didn't want to interrupt Molly's and Scott's private, romantic moment. Molly would tell me all about it later, I was sure. I quietly walked away from the football field and toward the old sports building, feeling better already. Since Molly and Scott were here, I didn't feel quite so alone.

The old sports building was mostly used for storage now. It had once been the offices for all of the sports coaches at Sunshine Springs High, but a few years ago the school district had decided to update the high school's facilities by building a brand-new, state-of-the-art sports complex with offices for the coaches, weight rooms, and other amenities. As far as I knew, the old building wasn't used for much more than storage these days. It was the perfect hiding place for Alice. She could stay warm and sheltered, but there weren't enough people coming by on a daily basis to notice that someone was squatting there.

I made my way into the building, surprised to see that it wasn't locked at all. Did the school just not bother locking it, or had Alice unlocked it for me from the inside? Either way, I was happy that I wouldn't have to fight my way in. I slipped into the musty front hallway and pushed away a shiver of worry.

I had no real reason to be afraid, right? As far as I knew, Alice was the only one in here. Besides, Scott and Molly weren't far away, and Mitch would be on his way as soon as he saw my message. Taking another deep breath, I made my way down the hallway, looking at the numbers on the office doors to see if I was getting any closer to the office number that Alice had given me. I found the right office relatively quickly, and opened the door slowly so I wouldn't startle her.

"Alice? Are you in there?"

A small sniffle answered me. My eyes took a moment to adjust to the windowless room, which was even darker than the hallway. When I was finally able to see what I was looking at, I saw Alice sitting in a corner of the room with her back against the wall and her knees up to her chest. She sniffled again, and gave me a small wave. I let out a sigh and went to sit beside her, putting an arm around her shoulders.

"Why are you doing this?" I asked. "I know this situation is stressful, but hiding isn't making things any better."

At that, Alice burst into sobs. "I know it looks horrible that I'm hiding, but I just can't handle all this pressure on me! And Sydney was bothering me. She kept showing up at my café, bothering my employees and asking where I was."

"Really?" My senses were instantly on high alert. "Why is she so interested in you and your café?"

"I don't know. I guess she was so upset by Trevor's death that she needed someone to blame, and I was the most likely person. When I learned that Norman had been killed too, I knew that Sydney would be harassing me about that as well. Not to mention the police were sure to have all sorts of questions for me. I couldn't stand the thought of it, and I decided it was time to disappear. I'd been thinking about doing that anyway, but as soon as Norman died I knew it was time."

I frowned as she spoke. Something about what she was saying made me uneasy. After thinking about it for a moment, I realized what it was.

"Wait a minute. How did you know Norman had been killed? You disappeared at almost the exact time that he died. How could you possibly have known what had happened before the police found you to tell you?"

A sense of dread slowly filled me. The most logical explanation for why Alice had so quickly known that Norman was dead was that she was the murderer. But that was absurd! She was Alice Warner, the sweet owner of the Morning Brew Café. There was no way she had killed not just Trevor, but Norman also.

If Alice noticed the dread on my face, she didn't let on that she had. She continued sobbing, seemingly oblivious to the horror and questions written into my expression.

"After I realized that I was a suspect in Trevor's murder case, I got myself a police scanner so I could keep track of what the police were doing. If they were coming after me, I wanted to know. So the moment that they called in Norman's murder on their radios, I knew. And even before they said it, I knew they'd be looking for me. I fled as quickly as possible. I'd already been thinking about places to hide, and I decided to come here right away before they could find me and question me again. I didn't commit either of these murders, and it's completely unfair that I'm being treated like some sort of criminal!"

I let out a sigh of relief. At least she had a logical explanation for how she'd known about Norman's murder. "Listen, Alice. I know it's unfair, but you have to work with the police here. The less you work with them, the worse off you'll be."

"No way. I'm not working with them. I know what they think about me. They think that because I'd let my liability insurance lapse when Trevor had threatened to sue me that I had a motive to get rid of him. They think that because Trevor was threatening to shut down my café that I had a reason to murder him. They're piling up all this supposed evidence against me, and they're going to convince a jury to put me away for life. I can't have that! Not when I'm innocent!"

"If you're innocent then the best thing you can do is work with Mitch. He truly believes you're innocent, too. The more you continue hiding out like this, the harder you're making it for him to help you."

Alice turned and glared at me. "What do you mean *if* I'm innocent? Don't tell me you're starting to believe everyone else who thinks I'm not!"

I shook my head. "I didn't mean it that way. I was speaking in a hypothetical sense."

But Alice was furious. I got the feeling that she was spoiling for a fight, and she pointed a finger right in my chest, her angry eyes flashing. "You shouldn't speak about this in a hypothetical sense. If you want someone to go after, then go after Sydney! Why is she so interested in this case? She tries to act like she's some sort of victim here because she was friends with Norman and Trevor. But lots of people were friends with Norman and Trevor. She doesn't get to act like she's the only one whose life has been turned upside down by all of this. If you ask me, I think she's a little too interested in this case. I think she's hiding something."

I wasn't going to disagree with Alice there. Sydney had indeed been acting strangely, and I believed she was more involved in this case than she was letting on. After all, she certainly hadn't mentioned to Mitch or anyone else on the night of the murder that she was romantically involved with Norman.

But whether or not Sydney was the guilty party here, it became apparent within about ten seconds that Alice was convinced that she was. Alice's voice continued to rise, and I instinctively tried to shush her. As far as I knew, there was no one else in this building. But the way things had been going lately, there might be a murderer around. I definitely didn't want to advertise my presence.

Thankfully, as soon as I tried to shush Alice, she seemed to lose steam. She put her face in her hands and dissolved into quiet sobs again.

I glanced down at my phone, trying to look at it without drawing Alice's attention. Where was Mitch? Had he still not gotten my voicemail? I understood that he needed time to focus and think about things for his work, but really, how could he stay so out of touch when there was a murderer on the loose? With a sigh, I decided that it was probably time for me to just contact the Sunshine Springs Police Department directly. I'd been hoping to avoid that, but I needed someone from the police department to get here before Alice completely lost it and decided to bolt again. The way she was acting right now, I had a feeling she might decide at any moment that she wanted to get out of here. And the next time she hid, she might hide far, far away from Sunshine Springs.

I was about to make some excuse to Alice about why I needed to step outside and make a phone call, but as I opened my mouth to speak, I was interrupted by a sudden crashing noise. It sounded like glass shattering— and not just a little bit of glass. The noise went on for several seconds. When it finally stopped, Alice and I looked at each other with wide eyes.

"What was that?" Alice asked, the fear evident in her voice. I wasn't exactly feeling too brave myself at the moment. What could possibly have caused such a giant crash? Then, after a few moments of silence, we heard the sound of loud cursing. The voice belonged to a man, but it was impossible to tell who. I felt a mixture of fear and hope. Was it possible that Mitch had arrived, and had somehow managed to knock over something glass that had been stored here?

I looked down at my phone, but still had no messages. That didn't necessarily mean anything. Mitch might have gotten my voicemail and rushed over without bothering to call me.

I hoped that was the case. If this wasn't him, then I didn't want to know who it was. Taking a deep breath, and telling myself to show some courage, I stood up.

"You stay here," I said to Alice. "And I mean it. Don't you dare move. If this person is out to get you, the worst thing you can do is take off running and screaming and completely give away your hiding spot. Understand?"

Alice looked up at me with eyes full of fear, and nodded. Praying that she would actually keep her promise, I took another deep breath and went to investigate.

I followed the sound of the cursing until I was standing right outside of the room the sound was coming from. I was pretty sure by now that Mitch wasn't the one who had accidentally knocked something over. The angry cursing didn't sound like Mitch's voice, although I couldn't tell who it was. It was definitely a man, and he was definitely furious. But beyond that, I had no clue. Surely, it wasn't the murderer. If someone had come in here intending to kill me or kill Alice, they wouldn't be making so much noise and giving themselves away.

I took a deep breath, deciding to just push the door open and see who it was. Most likely, it was someone who worked at the high school. They'd probably come into the storage area to get something and then accidentally knocked a bunch of stuff over. There was no reason for me to feel so terrified.

At the exact moment that I pushed the door open, I saw Alice running up beside me. I groaned. She hadn't listened to a single thing I'd said thus far in this investigation. I shouldn't have been surprised that she hadn't listened now, and had followed me toward the crashing noise instead of staying put like I'd asked. If I'd realized she was there a split-second earlier, I would have tried to get her to go back to her hiding spot before opening the door.

But it was too late now. The door was open, and the person in the room had surely noticed that they were no longer alone. After giving Alice a quick glare to let her know that I wasn't happy with her, I turned my attention back to the room. That's when I saw a sight so strange that it took me a few minutes to believe that I was actually seeing what I saw.

There, in the middle of the room, stood Cody Stringer—surrounded by piles of shattered glass and puddles of dark red liquid. For a moment, I worried that the liquid was blood. But there was no way. It wasn't exactly the right shade of red, and besides, it was far too much to be blood. It would have taken all the blood from about twenty human beings to make a puddle that big.

After staring in shock for a few moments, I realized what I was actually looking at. Behind Cody were several shelves, all of which appeared to be completely filled with cases of wine. Apparently, one of those shelves had been knocked over, and the wine bottles on that shelf had shattered. That had been the loud crash I'd heard, and the dark red liquid everywhere was the wine from the bottles that had shattered.

After a moment, I realized that Cody was staring at me in just as much shock as I was staring at him.

"What are you doing here?" I asked. "Why in the world is there a room of wine in an old high school sports building?"

Cody seemed to recover his senses when I spoke. He looked from Alice to me, glaring angrily. He didn't answer my question, which wasn't that surprising. Instead, he yelled back at me. "What are *you* doing here? This building is for school employees only."

Beside me, I heard Alice starting to whimper. Her nerves had already been horribly on edge, and now she was being yelled at by a crazy, angry man who was surrounded by piles of shattered glass and puddles of spilled wine. I couldn't blame her for being upset by the situation.

"Answer me!" Cody bellowed. "What are you doing here?"

I said the first thing that popped into my head, even though a nagging feeling at the back of my mind told me that I might be better off not talking to Cody at all and just trying to get out of there. "I was looking for Alice."

"And what was Alice doing here?" Cody demanded.

I balked again. What was I supposed to say? That she was hiding because she was wanted for murder. I knew Cody would have a few things to say about that, and they wouldn't be nice things. He was bound to get Alice all riled up again. How could I keep both Alice and Cody calm in this situation?

Apparently, I took too long to answer, and Cody's patience ran out. The next thing I knew, he had pulled a knife out of his pocket and was pointing it directly at me. "Answer me now, or you both die!"

The next thing I knew, I heard the sound of screaming. I realized the screaming was coming from Alice beside me, and then, I screamed myself. Cody had started charging toward me with the knife stretched out in front of him.

CHAPTER TWENTY

I only had seconds to figure out how to keep from being stabbed to death. Perhaps it wasn't the most elegant of solutions, but my gut instinct took over. Without thinking about it, I quickly jumped out of the way as Cody rushed toward me. This proved to be an effective strategy, at least for the moment. Instead of running into my chest with a knife, he ran straight into the wall behind me. The knife clattered to the floor, and I dove for it, hoping I could grab it before he got to it.

I wasn't so lucky. Cody managed to roll and grab it before me, then roll out of my reach. He hopped back to his feet and held the knife out in front of him.

"You're lucky!" he sneered. "If I'd gotten you a moment ago, that would have been the end of it. But I guess fate decided you deserve one more chance. So tell me, why are you here? Were you spying on me?"

I choked back the panic that was continuing to rise in my chest. "I'm not here to spy on you! I came to look for Alice."

Cody looked over at Alice, who was alternating between screaming and sobbing.

"Okay, fine then," he said. "Why was Alice spying on me?"

Alice only screamed, and then whimpered in response. Cody's patience seemed to run out again, and he looked like he was about to charge at Alice. But before I could completely panic, I suddenly heard a familiar voice from behind me.

"Hey! What's going on in here?"

I felt a rush of relief as I looked over my shoulder to see Scott approaching. Molly was with him, and while I certainly didn't want them tangled up in all of this danger, I had to admit that I had never been so glad to see them. I knew I couldn't have lasted much longer alone with Alice. But perhaps, with Scott and Molly here, we could hold Cody back until

Mitch got here with his officers.

Where was Mitch, anyway? Had he really not heard my voicemail yet? I was kicking myself over and over for not just calling 911. Why did I always try to prove that I knew how to handle things better than the police? Right now, I didn't care about proving anything. I only cared about surviving.

Cody swung his attention to Scott. "What are you doing here? What is this? Some sort of big party that I wasn't invited to?"

Scott looked over at the piles of glass and wine scattered across the floor and raised an eyebrow. "It looks like you're the one having a party in here."

This angered Cody, and he started lunging toward Scott. But Molly wasn't about to have any of that. She reached up as Cody rushed by, and then launched a punch into the side of his face. He staggered sideways and looked up at her in shock. Before he could react any further, she kicked the back of his knees to kick his legs out from under him. He fell onto the ground and landed in a pile of glass and wine, howling in pain as he did. When he tried to scramble to his feet, the sharp glass cut his arms and hands, and he started cursing and dropped the knife.

He quickly realized his mistake despite his pain, and tried to grab for the knife again. But Scott kicked it away, and Cody remained weaponless. Just as I let out a huge sigh of relief, I heard pounding footsteps running down the hallway.

Please let that be Mitch, I thought.

A moment later, my silent prayer was answered. Mitch appeared in the doorway of the room with his gun drawn. Several of his officers were behind him, looking just as ready for action. Mitch's eyes widened as he scanned the room, taking in the shattered wine bottles, Scott holding a knife, and the rest of us staring down at Cody's bloodied, angry figure.

"What is everyone doing here?" Cody yelled. "This building is only for use by school district employees and volunteers! You all have to get out of here right now!"

Mitch wasn't at all fazed by his outburst. "I could be wrong, but this looks like a crime scene, and the police have every right to be at a crime scene. Now, do you want to tell me what's going on, or should I arrest you and take you down to the station to get another statement?"

"I hate this town!" Cody yelled in response. "It's such an awful place. And Trevor and Norman deserved to die!"

My jaw dropped. Was Cody admitting to committing the murders?

"Regardless of how you feel about the town," Mitch said, "I'm going to disagree with you that Trevor and Norman deserved to die. Nobody deserves to die just for the fact that you didn't like them."

"There was a reason I didn't like them!" Cody yelled. "They were awful human beings who only wanted to be mayor of Sunshine Springs for their own benefit. They only cared about themselves!"

"Whether or not what you say is true," Mitch said, "Only caring about themselves is still not a reason for someone to deserve to die."

"You don't understand!" Cody yelled. "They were doing everything for their own gain. They would hurt or blackmail anyone in the process, and they didn't care. That's why I had to kill them! I didn't want to, but they left me no choice! They were trying to blackmail me."

My jaw dropped even further, and Alice started sobbing again.

"I knew it was you," Alice yelled. "You were trying to make everyone think that it was me because of how Trevor was threatening to sue over his chipped tooth. But it doesn't matter if Trevor had sued me, or even if I had lost everything! I would never kill someone! Norman and Trevor might not have been the nicest of people, but they didn't deserve this!"

That was all Alice could manage to say before she was sobbing too hard to get any more words out.

But Cody didn't have the chance to get any more words out, either. Before he could cast any more verbal jabs at Alice, Mitch was moving forward with a pair of handcuffs.

"Cody Stringer, you're under arrest for the murders of Trevor Truman and Norman Wade. You have the right to remain silent. Anything you say can and will be used against you in a court of law. You have the right to an attorney…"

I reached to put my arm around Alice as Mitch continued to recite Cody's rights to him.

"It's alright," I told her. "Cody can't hurt you now. Mitch will make sure of that."

Indeed, as soon as Mitch had gotten Cody properly cuffed, he came over to check on Alice.

"Are you alright?" he asked, deep concern filling his voice.

"Oh, it's so awful!" she said. "I just can't believe everything that's happened."

With that, she dissolved into sobs again and collapsed into Mitch's arms. Mitch coughed awkwardly, unsure of how to handle the situation. Finally, he settled on patting Alice's back a bit clumsily as she sobbed into his chest.

Meanwhile, Cody was screaming in the background, still telling the police that they had no right to be there and that he'd had every right to kill Norman and Trevor because they'd completely deserved it.

I shook my head in disbelief, then glanced over at Molly and Scott. They looked just as bewildered by the whole thing as I felt. I still had a lot of questions: Why, exactly, had Cody done this? It had to have been more than just the simple fact that he didn't like Norman and Trevor. And what was with the wine? Why had Cody been ordering huge cases of wine and storing them here in the old high school building?

I didn't have time to figure out the answers right now, though. Molly was pulling me toward her and lifting her cell phone up.

I groaned. "Not again!"

Molly grinned at me. "Yes, again! I've got to get another selfie for my 'murderers being arrested' photo album."

I continued to think that the whole idea of an album full of selfies with people being arrested for murder was completely ridiculous, but I humored Molly and smiled as she put her right arm around me and lifted her cell phone in the air with her left hand.

It wasn't until she was lowering her hand that I saw the giant diamond on the ring finger of her left hand. In the midst of all the excitement of finding Alice and nearly being killed by Cody, I had completely forgotten about the fact that everyone had been expecting Scott to propose to Molly that night. My mouth dropped open again, this time for a good reason. In my excitement, I was once again at a loss for words. All I could do was point at the ring on Molly's hand.

She grinned at me and held out her hand for me to see. "Yep. I'm engaged. It's been quite a night, hasn't it?"

"Indeed it has," I said as I glanced over at Cody being dragged out of the room, and then looked back at Molly's sparkling diamond. "Indeed it has."

CHAPTER TWENTY-ONE

Molly came in to the Drunken Pie Café early the next morning to have breakfast with me and catch up on things. It had been a late night, with all of us heading down to the station to give official statements, and we'd been too tired after all of that to do anything other than head home and go to bed. But now that I'd slept a few hours—there was nothing like knowing the murderer had been caught to help me sleep like a baby—I was ready to hear everything about the proposal.

Molly was only too happy to describe everything in great detail. "He planned a picnic out on the football field to commemorate our first kiss. Do you remember when I told you about that?"

I nodded with a grin. "That's the first thing I thought of when I saw you out there last night."

"Yes, well, he said that he'd never told me before, because he was embarrassed to admit to it, but that I was actually his first kiss ever. Then he told me that he wanted me to be his last kiss. He took me back to the high school football field where it all began to tell me that he wants to be with me to the end."

Molly's eyes sparkled with tears of happiness, and I reached over to squeeze her hand. "See? I told you he'd figure out something romantic."

She nodded. "You were right. It was so romantic! He even had Theo make bottles of wine with specially printed labels that had our names and the date of our first kiss on them."

"He remembers the actual date of the kiss?"

Molly nodded. "He knew it was the homecoming football game our junior year of high school. He went back and figured out what day that was, and then had the labels made. And, of course, he ordered me my current favorite pie from your café. In a way, we have you to thank for the fact that we got back together. It was because you came to town and met both of us that Scott and I started hanging out again. Without you bringing us together again, we might not have realized that that small spark that had been there all those years ago was still there."

I smiled. "I was happy to play a part in this, however small that part might have been."

"It was a very important part," Molly insisted. "Oh! And I almost forgot to tell you: he also gave me a beautiful, limited-edition print of Jane Austen's complete works. He knows how much I love her, and he wanted me to know that he'll support my passions and help build up the town's library in whatever way he can."

I grinned at her. "Well, it sounds like you've already figured this out, but I'll say it anyway: he sounds like a keeper."

"He's definitely a keeper. I'm so happy! And now, I have a question for you, Izzy. Would you be my maid of honor?"

I gasped, and my heart filled with joy. I hadn't been sure if Molly would want me to fill that role for her. Yes, we were best friends now, but we hadn't been best friends for that long. I wasn't sure if there was some other woman in Molly's life to whom Molly might feel obligated to offer the role. But apparently, Molly didn't feel obligated to do anything except ask me to take on that honor.

"Of course!" I exclaimed, and threw my arms around her, nearly knocking her coffee over in the process. "I would be honored."

For about half an hour after that, Molly and I discussed preliminary wedding plans. I wasn't generally a big fan of weddings after the huge divorce I'd gone through, but for Molly, I would put aside that hang-up. I was truly excited for her, and I wanted her wedding day to be the fairytale she'd always dreamed of.

But our wedding planning was cut short when I heard a sharp rap at my café's door. I looked up, startled, wondering if it was time to open already and if I had people waiting outside eager for their morning pie and coffee. But there were still about twenty minutes until I opened, and the rapping wasn't from a customer. Instead, it was from Mitch and Theo. I grinned, and went to let them in.

"I'm surprised I haven't heard from you this morning," Mitch said to me. "I half expected you to be beating down the police station's door, asking me to explain what exactly had happened in this case."

I grinned at him. "I was trying not to bother you. But since you're here now, I am sort of dying to know what happened."

"Well, we got a full confession from Cody. Turns out, he was involved in a scheme to sell alcohol to minors."

"Really?" I asked, my brain already scrambling to understand how that tied into the murder.

"Yep," Theo said. "Remember I told you that Cody had placed quite a few special orders? It turns out those cases of wine weren't for events Trevor was putting on as part of his campaign. Instead, Cody had figured out a way to sell bottles of wine to local high schoolers."

My eyes widened. "So that's why everyone on the football team loved him!"

"Exactly," Theo said. "And it was the only reason that he coached football at the local high school. He didn't care about giving back to the community. He cared about finding customers, and most of the football team was all too happy to take him up on his offer to give them easy access to alcohol."

"No wonder Sammy was so afraid of getting in trouble when I went to talk to him," I said. "He must have thought I knew something about the wine, and that he was going to get in trouble if I figured out the details."

"Sammy wasn't the only one afraid of getting in trouble for all this," Mitch said. "It turns out that Trevor had figured out what Cody was doing, and had threatened to out him to the police. Selling alcohol to minors is a felony, so it would have been quite a big deal if Cody had been found out. Rather than risk having a horrible criminal record and never being able to work as a campaign manager again, Cody freaked out and decided the easiest thing to do was to kill Trevor and try to make it look like an accident. Unfortunately, he botched the job and it was clear that Trevor hadn't drowned by accident. But luckily for Cody, Trevor had been arguing with Alice so much that it was easy enough to blame Alice—especially since she'd been hiding in the bathroom during the timeframe of Trevor's murder and didn't have a solid alibi."

I frowned. "But I thought Cody himself had an alibi for that night. You said it was rock-solid."

Mitch shrugged sheepishly. "It wasn't as rock-solid as I thought it was. It turned out that the high-schoolers who vouched for him had only done so because they didn't want him to get in trouble. Obviously, if his scheme was exposed then they would also be exposed as illegally buying alcohol. So they lied and said he'd been inside the whole time, even though he hadn't. They'll be in some trouble themselves, although obviously not nearly as much trouble as Cody."

"And what about Norman?" Molly asked. "Why did he kill Norman?"

"He was worried that Norman had also discovered the scheme to sell alcohol to minors," Mitch explained. "You already know, of course, that Cody had discovered that Norman and Sydney were committing election fraud. But when Norman snuck into Cody's office and tried to steal all of that evidence, he accidentally disturbed some papers related to the alcohol sales. Cody freaked out and thought that Norman had discovered the alcohol scheme and was going to use it to force Cody to keep the election fraud silent. Cody snuck into Norman's office to try to steal any information back. That's who you saw coming in the night you went to find the files Norman had stolen."

I shook my head slowly. "I went through Norman's entire office, but I don't remember seeing anything related to selling alcohol to minors."

Mitch nodded. "As far as we can tell, Norman never actually found any information on the scheme. But it was quite unfortunate for him that Cody thought he had, because Cody decided that he had to take Norman out as well. He was in so deep at that point that he must have figured one more murder was no big deal."

I felt sick to my stomach. "No big deal!? It was one more life needlessly ended."

"I agree," Mitch said. "But as you saw last night, Cody didn't exactly feel that way. He took out Norman, and we think he might have been planning to kill Sydney as well. He thought it would be easy to blame all of that on Alice, since Sydney had reacted so strongly against Alice when she discovered Norman was dead. At any rate, things are settled now. We have a confession from Cody that he killed Norman and Trevor, and we have a confession from Sydney about the election fraud. Hopefully this will be the end of the current murder spree in Sunshine Springs."

"I certainly hope so," I said, still feeling a little bit sick. "I can't believe that Cody did all of that."

Before anyone could reply, we were interrupted by another rap at the door. I looked up to see Grams standing there with Sprinkles and Alice. I hurried to let them in, and Grams threw her arms around my neck. "Izzy! You did it again! You solved the case. I'm so proud of you!"

I blushed. "I'm not sure it's accurate to say I solved it. I definitely had a lot of help from Mitch on this one."

Mitch cracked his knuckles and gave me a broad smile. "I have to admit that you helped out quite a bit. If you hadn't figured out that Alice was at the high school and then found Cody, who knows if we would have ever caught him. He was getting ready to make a break for it, and if he'd left town, we might never have connected the dots on all of this. I'm truly thankful for your help. You know I don't like you working on these cases, but I must confess that your help turned out to be a good thing this time."

Sprinkles jumped excitedly around me, barking as if to add his own praise to the compliments everyone had already given me. I blushed deeper, but then I noticed that I wasn't the only one blushing. As I looked up again, I saw Mitch and Alice exchanging a glance that looked quite flirty. Instantly, I remembered Alice giving Mitch a giant hug the night before. Was it possible that the hug had sparked something between them? I glanced over at Molly to see if she had noticed it, but she was too busy petting Sprinkles. Mitch looked over at me at that moment and caught my eye, then quickly looked away again.

That was all the answer I needed. Mitch wasn't the type to look away from anyone, so he was definitely feeling like he had a secret to hide. Was it what I thought it was? From the looks on his and Alice's faces, I had a feeling that there might soon be another new couple in Sunshine Springs.

I smiled happily, and looked over at Theo to see if he knew anything about this. He winked at me, but I couldn't tell from that wink whether he knew anything or not. I'd have to watch Mitch closely over the next few weeks, but it looked like I might be down to just one man in Sunshine Springs who was chasing after me: Theo.

Too bad I wasn't interested in dating that one man. I was, however, glad to see my other friends finding happiness.

Alice started passing out the muffins she'd baked for us, and even though I already had pie and didn't need any more breakfast, I happily wolfed some muffins down. I could never say no to Alice's delicious breakfast muffins.

We all chatted a bit more about the murder case, but there wasn't that much more to say. Cody had been caught, and Trevor and Norman would at least have justice. The world had one less criminal on the streets, and I knew we would all sleep better because of that.

The clock kept ticking forward, and soon it was time for everyone to get to work. Molly took off to go to the library, Alice took off to go to her café, Mitch needed to get down to the police station, and although Grams didn't have to work, she did have an appointment at Sophia's Salon for her and Sprinkles.

"Go have fun, Sprinkles," I said to my Dalmatian. "I can't wait to see what color your nails are when you get back."

I found to my surprise that I actually meant that. I had come to accept the way that Grams liked to push her own fashion sense on my dog. Sprinkles seemed to enjoy it, and who was I to hold him back from a good time?

That left only Theo as I unlocked the door for a day of business.

"Sticking around for more pie?" I asked.

Theo grinned at me. "Nope, but I would like a glass of wine. I don't care that it's only nine A.M. You don't judge your customers right?"

"No, I don't," I said as I poured him a giant glass of wine. "And after the night we've all had, I think you deserve it. I take it Mitch took a statement from you about the wine sales?"

"He did. And I feel horrible that my wine was being used for a scheme like that."

"Don't feel horrible. You had no way of knowing. Besides, it's sure to get you some notoriety in town, don't you think?"

Theo groaned. "I don't need any notoriety. I'm quite happy with things the way they are. I get enough attention just for being the richest man in town. Although, I don't get as much attention as I'd like from you." He winked at me in that way he often did that said he was mostly joking, but if I seriously wanted attention from him, he was happy to give it.

I winked back. "Sorry, but you know I'm not in the market for a boyfriend right now."

"Too busy solving murder cases?" he teased.

I sighed. "I would like to say I'm done with those, but I've said that several times before and it never quite seems to be the case. But really, with Christmas coming up, I do hope that I get a rest from sleuthing so I can focus on holiday sales."

Theo grinned at me. "You never know what Christmas will bring. It is a time of high emotion. Of course, I'm hoping that emotion translates into romance."

He winked at me once more, and this time I rolled my eyes at him. "I might murder *you* if you don't get out of my café now," I told him. "I'm going to have customers in here in a few minutes, and I don't need you distracting me from them."

Theo laughed, reached over to squeeze my arm affectionately, and then left. I had to admit I was a little sad to see him go. I did enjoy his company, but it was true that I was busy with the pie shop, and I had a lot to do with Christmas coming up.

For now, there were no murders to be solved, and there was a lot of pie to be baked and sold. Business was in full swing for the Drunken Pie Café, and I was extraordinarily grateful for that. Even though I was sometimes so busy that I couldn't breathe, I wouldn't have had it any other way.

If you asked me, life in Sunshine Springs was pretty much perfect.

ABOUT THE AUTHOR

Diana DuMont lives and writes in Northern California. When she's not reading or dreaming up her latest mystery plot, she can usually be found hiking in the nearby redwood forests. You can connect with her at www.dianadumont.com.

Printed in Great Britain
by Amazon

32621922R00076